1919—A Kansas Tale

DATE DUE

JAN 0 4 2013			
GAYLORD			P

1919—A Kansas Tale

Dorothy Dierks Hourihan

VANTAGE PRESS
New York

Cover design by Dorothy Dierks Hourihan

FIRST EDITION

Copyright © 2010 by Dorothy Dierks Hourihan

Published by Vantage Press, Inc.
419 Park Ave. South, New York, NY 10016

Manufactured in the United States of America
ISBN: 978-0-533-16311-3

Library of Congress Catalog Card No: 2009910985

0 9 8 7 6 5 4 3 2 1

I dedicate this book to the memory of my husband, my perfect partner in life and love, Timothy Francis Hourihan. His spirit continues to inspire me to create with both paint and words. The dazzling grace, brilliance, and wit that were his are seldom known and remain an important part of all who knew him.

Introduction

Any explanation of my intention to explore drama in this story is best understood by considering the French impressionists, painters whose visions clothed some particular subjects with the "main character" of their style, atmosphere.

Although this story contains sketches of characters in rustic early twentieth-century Kansas, the "leading role" is America in the first part of that century, shaped around World War I, women's suffrage, racism and prejudice, all to the rhythms of America's original jazz. If some of the grandeur of, and humanity in, our land, at a time of continuing expansion, is communicated with some lyricism and humor, I have succeeded.

1

Premature Denouement

Burnt orange and glowing cadmium triggered disbelief on that Kansas night, October 1919. Eighteen was Ned's age. Nan was a year younger. Ned's face, already with some leathering from earlier Oklahoma field work, seemed basted from heat through his instinct to rush to blazing silhouettes. The small house was all but gone, mere black chalk and smoked framing. Nan's family was dead, the firemen said, standing in the hot colors which had been a backdrop to the horizon only a few hours before, when the two teenagers had set out on a date ... a pumpkin sunset, an autumn walk, ice cream sodas, and gatherings in the park with schoolmates. Now firemen quickly moved two stretchers from the front yard onto carts as Nan attempted to remove blankets covering the burned and suffocated dead. One firefighter held a small body wrapped in sheets as the teenager rushed to grab her younger sister. She gasped in protest.

"No ... no, there is a mistake and I have to see ... I have to look at my little Katie, and my Mama and Daddy."

Nan pressed both hands hard against her temples as she spun around to take in the spread of fire. Nothing beyond the house was burning. The garage, with its attached workroom out back, was standing. A gas explosion was mentioned ... her head was swirling. A smell, not of fall fires or leaves burning, but a thick choking scent of gloom, made breathing an effort.

She moved toward the two stretchers but stumbled and

was lifted by Ned who was unable to understand his own inertia. Neighbors were standing near in the dark when Mrs. Wilkins from across the street touched Nan's shoulder.

"You can stay with us until you have a place or settle somewhere," she said.

This woman had never been friendly, and in the small town where most people worked for very modest incomes she was considered to be shabby. Her small children were wild and unmannerly and her husband, who was known to drink too much, stood behind his wife, peering at the fire, smelling of hard alcohol and barn droppings. Nan instinctively withdrew, still gazing at the diminished frame structure. Most of the beams had crumbled. The tin roof now covered what was left of fallen understructures and furnishings, all burning in the small basement. Porch posts still stood, smoking and charcoal black as a ludicrous entry to nothing. The same was true of a back stoop with wooden steps which sizzled as the firemen's water, some thrown from leather buckets, attacked to smother flames. Lacking a steam engine truck, the firemen always had water pumped from the river on hand in the truck's water tank. On this night they hand-pumped through the hoses, managing to turn the blazes into smoking embers.

"Thank you, but I'll be going to my aunt's house ... if the firemen ... will take me."

These words, uttered in stuttering desperation to avoid the neighbor, seemed to suck energy from Nan's body. Her knees gave way. Ned grabbed her before she hit the ground, as he asked volunteer firemen to give them a ride out to the Quinn place. Nan had to be restrained from getting into the ambulance which held the bodies ... she saw the transport move away into the dark and ran after it. Ned ran along with her for a hundred yards until her breathing became asthmatic and the fire truck had pulled up for them.

Shaking and shivering in the crisp air as the open truck

2

sped ahead, Nan clung to Ned's waist. Volunteers, still pumping water from the horse-drawn fire wagon onto sizzling ruins, remained as the undertaker's carrier moved further away. An ambulance left with the bodies as Nan mumbled, "I can't go ... I can't go to anyone ... what'll I do ... can't go ... my aunt doesn't like me, hates my family ... my family is ... no more, anymore. I don't have a family ... I have no folks! Oh, Ned ... what'll I do?"

Ned felt the cold tears flowing through his shirt. Her body seemed too frail now to even quiver, but he held her tightly for fear she would shake herself out of the truck. The deep laughter and frolicking enjoyed by these two when the moon was high, just a few blown leaves ago, was the top end of a seesaw ride, blissful play which now dropped into hell, all in one evening, precipitating doubts that both ends were of the same life. Haunting questions of where they had been at the moment the fire swelled, and raged, and killed, occupied Ned's mind with wondering as a defense against screaming. Had they been riding wildly on the dirt roads which skirted the river? He would be quiet for Nan.

Ella Quinn, estranged sister of Nan's mother, hurried out of the front door upon hearing the truck pull up to her place. She was heavy-boned and appeared fatter than she was.

"Glory be to God! What's going on at this time of night?"

"Miss Ella, we have bad news. The Heath house burned down. They're all dead except your niece here. We've brought her to stay with you." The fireman spoke less sympathetically than apologetically.

"Impossible! I'm sick. I have the flu with infection and we don't want to start another epidemic. Mr. Hahn already made so much money on that nightmare parade of coffins being hauled down the roads day and night. How could the house burn? No lightning ... no smokers there ... are you sure my sister is dead? Where are the bodies? Oh, me!"

3

Ella glared vacant-eyed at her niece while wailing and coughing into a stooping position to vomit, but then the spinster jerked herself up with arms akimbo, only to say, "Away now! Burned down? The little house could burn quickly but even as the last house in that so-called neighborhood ... on the edge of the block and alley ... where were neighbors? What time was it that you couldn't pull them out? My family made it through the flu ... now this ... away now! You'll get what I've got and die yourselves. You'll all be sick. I'm too sick to help ... don't much know the girl ... my poor sister, oh no, my sister! My niece can go to some of those Mormon types. I'll pay. Pay for the expenses of the burials. I'll tell Hahn in the morning."

Ella shouted this as an afterthought, over her shoulder, and walked swiftly as possible, with a slight limp, acquired in childhood sliding down icy snow off the Quinn's bar roof, towards the open front door where the outline of another female figure could be discerned. The two slammed the heavy door, leaving the night callers aghast.

"I've never heard such a thing! Is she loony? Your own flesh and blood has no feelings ... is she crazy? Is she just a devil? Can you men drive us to Mr. Hahn's house?" Ned said. "I work for him. He's generous and kind. Anyway, he'll be taking care of burials for us and we'll get some advice. Since this girl has no other relatives Mrs. Hahn will put her up for the night. She'll be all right. We'll be all right."

A Negro woman came running from the corner of the farmhouse towards Nan. Having heard the fireman deliver the news, she cried out, "I raised yo mama, chile, and you can be with us in the back cabin for as long as you want."

"Not tonight, Sadie," Ned said. As gloom, a deeper darkness than visual, had closed over Nan's lavender eyes this teenager took her hand and whispered, "I'll always take care of you."

No decision would be so carved in stone for the next sixty years, nor would vivid fears, passions, or emotions, tapped by births, deaths, joys or grief, match the heavy pounding in Ned's chest as he left the Hahn's big house to walk their property a quarter-mile to his small digs above the funeral parlor to grab a sweater, as the night was turning colder, and then into the night again to retrieve his mare, Mollie, from the place where he had tied her to avoid letting the Heaths know of the night ride. Ned revisited images of the evening. Leaving Nan's home at dusk the two schoolmates hurried to a nearby woods where Ned's horse had been tied. A fast gallop into the town's only junction was reached quickly so the town's high school population would believe he had actually gotten this mysterious beauty to spend time with him. Impatient to have her to himself, and after some laughs with friends over ice cream, Ned pulled his date up behind him on his mare to trot away from the group. Enough socializing, enough sharing of this long-awaited time with the girl he already adored. Now he would have her hold to his chest and speak into his ear, then in a slow walk the two could speak of Nan's love of music, his love of poetry, and, if lucky, he might secure her consent to spend time with him again. The night ride took them farther than he intended; far from the outskirts of the town, when, squinting at his wristwatch in the moonlight, and before finishing their fun at rollicking, Ned gave a kick to show what the fast gait could do with two friends straddling. A hardened dirt road edging the little town met hoofs for a percussive clipping rhythm to thrill the girl's spirit despite her fear of speed. This was her first date. Ned was known as the fastest horseman in town, so the mare had been hidden to avoid giving Mr. Heath an opportunity to find any reason to mistrust the caller's respect for his daughter's safety. Even the stroll from the woods to the Heath house was enchanting to the boy. They had not smelled smoke, nor even heard the fire wagon which seemed to have alerted and drawn a crowd to the fire site. Ned shivered late into the night, alone with a now-pervasive feeling of responsibility. It was all up to him ... no time for falling in love and no privilege of romance and dreams. Their only assets ... two strong and lovely bodies and fine minds ... gifts which would support them far longer than the average life given to others born in the years of their births. Their contemporaries would average lives of less than fifty years while Ned and Nan would both reach octogenarian status.

The town was called Flat Rock. By 1919 it owned up to housing over a thousand residents, who still thought of themselves as frontiersmen, even though the ongoing Washington census would be reporting the country's population to be growing rapidly. The Kansas River made land fertile, with gentle rolling terrain beckoning earlier settlers to stop here and start life again. Shallow brooks and deeper waterways meandered from the river. Flat and open spaces produced corn and timber. City slickers outnumbered farm folk, with the number of farm families having fallen below thirty percent of the overall population of the United States. There was some sentiment in cities that this was for the best since illiteracy had dropped to six percent and life expectancy had risen to fifty-four years from forty-nine. Work in urban areas was plentiful. The country, producing two-thirds of the world's oil supply, gave mobility to approximately fifteen million registered automobiles, but even with such reports people of Kansas looked with no envy on city life and were intent on remaining westward, enjoying a life of space and privacy. Entering the Union in 1861 as a free state, Kansas had overcome its tendencies to side with slavery, but the KKK had not altogether disappeared. In Flat Rock churches were more numerous than needed. Baptist, Episcopal, Methodist and Lutheran denominations served the community, while some traveled to worship as they chose. Here no Indians, no Jews, one Catholic family and one Negro couple resided ... a sleepy little place, seemingly, but not with paucity of universal resentments, discontents, ambitions, aggressions ... all breeding grounds, hopefully, for a balancing of inevitable love and hate. No human community has, or ever will escape the fate, the one-way uncoiling of both despair and jubilance. Flat Rock would see it all.

Upon waking, still in his smoky clothes. Ned planned with Mr. Heath for the three funerals. The night before Mrs. Hahn had sensitively accompanied Nan into a small and cozy bedroom on the third floor of their large farmhouse, and having raised five daughters of her own, was at ease in telling Nan that she would not be left alone. When the young girl's sobbing shook the bed throughout the night the older woman simply reached to touch Nan's shoulder saying, "I'm here, I'm with you ... you are not alone." Nan had no one, although somewhere in the East were relatives of her mother's parents, Ted Quinn and Lizzy Seltzer. She was left with only Ella Quinn who wanted little if anything to do with her. Ned had no one in this place. He loved her, and she needed him. The Hahns instructed Ned to help the orphan through the burials. Only then, with Nan's acceptance, would they support his plan to become her husband, her family ... and her protector if she chose.

Ella Quinn had already called Ralph Hahn to assure him he would get his money for all services for the Heaths. Knowing Ella had a fat purse and paid promptly, Ralph simply said, "You know I will see to it that this girl has dignity in the care of her parents and sister ... now you know this as well as the other six party-line listeners nosing in on the telephone line!"

Nan's mother, Bess Heath, having graduated from secondary school, had been chosen by the community teacher to assist in the tutoring of children. When the position of postmistress was available she was hired. This fiery-tempered redhead with dancing blue eyes and slender body was much too wild to be matched with the preacher. She struggled to be soft and demure, but her great spurts of laughter tainted with sarcasm exhibited the irony and contradiction of her inner dualism ... liberal spirit and rigid mind. Those gathered at the gravesides that dreary fall afternoon were there for her, having viewed her husband, the preacher, as much too judgmental and austere, and knowing how he held reins on the three females at a time when the country was fast changing by two movements, both teetering on fast-forward gears. One was the national, and European, growing sympathy for support of women's suffrage, and the other, rapid advancement of federal aid to road building all across the country, bringing mobility, curiosities, and liberalizing sentiments. His rules were well known by all ... no Coca-Cola, no dancing, no smoking, quiet Sundays, and hard work every day. Bess's paternal grandparents had lived in Baltimore. Her mother's relatives were from Georgia and before that from North Carolina.

Mr. Heath had come from the other direction ... from out of the West ... and brought no kin. He was skilled at survey work and in the small town, as something of a mystery, was demarcated by what was read as his advanced schooling. He traveled as a Mormon preacher with no church building or congregation as held in other more established sects. There was only a handful of Mormons in the town, hence they traveled with the Heaths to countryside farm houses to reach families for Sunday services which were held in homes or buildings. His wife and two daughters sang and played an organ when one was available. The design of his mission was not unique to his chosen church, as both preachers and teachers, were often travelers in search of followers in the Midwest. Some friends and converts attended the funeral, but news traveled slowly. Many did not hear of the burning until too late. Unlike times when tornados hit the Midwest, when neighbors would arrive quickly to rebuild houses and barns in Kansas and Illinois, the Heath's home would not be rebuilt by friends.

As a young boy Tom Heath found himself in Nebraska with parents from New England who educated him in the classics, critical thinking and logic, and who both contacted influenza long before the so-called Spanish flu epidemic. At their passing, when the boy was only fifteen, he learned simple trades and read avidly, without pressure to earn money since the Heaths had bought land which the boy could sell off slowly over three years with money left over to move elsewhere. A Mormon minister found Tom wounded on a trail near the northern Kansas border after being thrown from a train by robbers as he was on his way to study at the University of Kansas. The preacher pulled Tom up behind him on this horse, transporting him to the Mormon family home where he could be nursed back to health.

Outlaws were attracted to helpless victims on trains who would give up their jewelry and money at the point of a gun. Many Easterners had withdrawn all of their money from banks and headed West on trains only to suffer losses. Tom had resisted and retained deep scars on his head for life from the attack on the train. Having had no experience with organized religion he was moved emotionally by the rescuer's quiet spirit and enormous physical strength. The man stood six-foot five inches and was a fine raconteur in the evenings, when the preacher's wife and children and Tom gathered in the homestead to hear parables and personal dramas. Tom was enraptured and soon became a student of the master. During some months of recovery Tom became an assistant to his lifesaver. The older and younger man were an energized team; one with humor and wining ways, the younger a serious designer of words on Christian tenets. The two never addressed each other by name, but by Lad and Teacher. As often as not, tablets which initially held Tom's introductions to sermons evolved into free lines, then contour lines crying for shading to give life to chiaroscuro and definition to familiar forms of landscape, or the faces of the preacher's family. Lad's several years with Teacher brought the gifts of development of a hard body from farm labor and of a mind for his chosen profession. These years, and years following, failed to bring clarity to his mind as to why a Divine Creator had not given equality of life to all humans or equal dignity and respect to artists and church leaders. The Bible did not address these questions. Although the New Testament insists on "inclusion" at the base of Christian teachings, the greatest book ever written, Old or New, did not address equality, the condition of the dead, or the awesome concept of an endless universe among endless universes. Tom was a believer not by blind faith as Teacher had been, but through his very private, taciturn and constant questioning. Feeling committed to his religion he set out on his own mission after several years with Teacher.

2

Burials

A threatening sky hung low as the funeral procession set out. Tom and Bess Heath's bodies were carried in a remodeled 1914 Bessemer truck, one of many which had been used in the work of the Automobile Trail Blazing Association to transport men in the service of marking a through trail by painting telegraph poles all the way from New York to the Pacific Coast. This truck had broken down in the process of painting markings in 1918, just north of Flat Rock, which, like every town in America, had a Ford garage. It had been hauled in for repair when Ralph Hahn, upon spotting it, convinced the mechanic to give the driver such a high estimate to fix the truck that the driver gladly sold the damaged goods to Hahn for a pittance. Ralph had a vision for the truck ... a transformation into a hearse, with side enclosures, rear extension, plush interior and high-gloss black exterior finish. No Easterner would have recognized it as a former work truck. The girl's body was transported in a shiny white horse-drawn buckboard wagon. Ned drove himself and Nan in the town-owned ambulance, with blessings of the sheriff.

From Flat Rock the burial ground was a fifteen-minute drive by automobile but double that by horse ... the procession seemed interminable under a sky overcast with storm threats. Nan wondered whether the long transport, because of the child's wagon, was more painful, extending the terror and anguish of the final lowering of what she knew as

11

warm bodies, senses, and reactions with powers and dignity of minds and expressions ... or, a swift brief ride cheating one of pain and shocking disbelief at the final lowering, the ugly reality of human extinction. The longer ride seemed better to her. The graveyard was a half-hour into Kansas City by auto, depending on whether the dirt roads were dry or muddy. Nan knew that her father had traveled into the city regularly on business ... his energies always seeming endless. Now at this midpoint between city and village were many of the schoolmates of Nan and Katie, and most of the townspeople. Ella stood very close to the local Episcopal minister, directing her gravelly voice to Hahn, saying, "Get rid of the shovels ... is this the dignity you promised this orphan?"

Otis and Sadie, the Negro couple who had served the Quinns as tenants and workers, on their place since the Quinns had made their home in Flat Rock, placed themselves behind Ella. These two had seen the births of Ella and Bess and wept bitterly.

Soil removed to create the rectangular six-foot spaces for the dead was piled high round three sides of each opening. The coffins were placed on the cleared sides with underroping for lowering. Ned quickly removed the shovels and returned to stand near Nan. Her father had put Tennyson's poems in her hands during the summer.

With the rich earth smell bringing memories of fine corn growing, she struggled to silently recite her favorite line from "In Memoriam,"

Behold, we know not anything;
   I can but trust that good shall fall
At last--far off--at last, to all,
And every winter change to spring.

Should these words be carved on her father's tombstone, or at least more than a name and dates? No, she thought, it would not be Christian. Nan couldn't know that over the next sixty years she would learn little more about life or death than hope ... and yet compile a continuous medley of immediate and distant tactics for survival ... reaching for some joys in each present hour. Nan asked herself what could be the epitaph for a twelve-year-old, what summation could be appropriate as her sister entered the threshold to a new existence or nothingness? Suddenly a smile curled Nan's lips as she reviewed images of this little girl, by which she would be remembered. Katie had inherited her father's large green eyes, which were her great pride, since she adored him, and tried desperately to make drawings which would please him. She had, it seemed, pencil and crumpled paper in her pockets at all times, available for sketching anything she might view as beautiful. Once, Nan had been sent to find Katie as a long summer day was ending. It was not like Katie to be far from the house so Nan began to look in small nearby open lots or meadows when she heard a small voice singing and smoke rising from a dugout that some boys had made. Nan peered into the opening to see the younger girl in a deeper adjoining open ditch with a multitude of matches strewn on the red-clay floor, the result of attempts to get a Havana Cuban cigar, stolen from her father's bedside table, to catch fire and give rise to smoke for joining overhead cloud formations, under a cerulean blue sky ceiling. This was the vision she hoped some day to paint. As she manipulated smoke patterns she visualized her first canvas. Delighted, as her little bare feet cooled in the damp mud in the hot Kansas season, she was suddenly disturbed by her sister's discovering her secret. This had been her first private hour, free of adult watching and adult awareness as her heartbeat accelerated in identification with her father whom she knew also smoked secretly! Nan pulled her out of the ditch to straighten her clothes and wipe her clean of dirt, swearing to keep the event to herself. As the sisters entered the kitchen it was not unusual for Katie's summer feet to leave tracks of mud across the floor, but, surprisingly, the smell of the tobacco from her long blonde pigtails and the blue face she wore from inhaling smoke was mentioned by no one at the supper table. The family knew the young girl was eccentric--it was just the way she was. The skinny yet tough "tomboy" had put to shame both boys and girls, her age and older, through her skill with the yoyo toy, with her performance of the "round the world" trick, the "rock the baby in the cradle" maneuver, and by holding the longest "hesitation" spin as she threw the yoyo down and then, when no one believed she could possibly finally tweak it up into her palm, she did! At the big Flat Rock picnics on her grandfather's farm, more than once Katie had brought out her enviable collection of gorgeous agates to knock out all the marbles from the center of the ring, drawn in dirt, before anyone else even had a turn at it. Nan smiled wider now, remembering how her little sister's knees were, each summer, rough and scarred from kneeling on the ground. Nan saw, with her near-perfect visual recall, Tennyson's "Sleeping Beauty" lines;

She sleeps; her breathings are not heard
    In palace chambers far apart,

She sleeps, nor dreams, but ever dwells
    A perfect form in perfect rest.

Katie would not see her menses. She would never know a body experience gifted for new life. Nan knew her Bible, remembering that disciples had not addressed the condition of the dead before Judgment Day ... only 2 Corinthians taught that when absent from the body one is present with the Lord.

Nan had sensed her father's occasional questioning of his belief and had gained it herself as though through osmosis.

The orphan's only reality seemed to be the sudden rainfall. Her thoughts floated above the weeping mentality of friends attending, and above the dull hum of the visiting minister's voice, so unlike her father's beguiling deliveries on all celebrations of life or death. Would these folks rush from a drenching in the chill October air? Would they run from the chill or from the horror of the grim's reaper's unspeakable mistake? Nan prayed she was dreaming ... that she would be in her home tonight. Her mother would hold her, she would hold to her sister, and Tom Heath would comfort them all. Perhaps the electric flashes and storm would simply wash away God's gaffe!

3

Discoveries

Nan stayed with the Hahns for several weeks, returning to the home property to search, with Ned, for anything in the ruins. Her mother's car, a red 1906 Cadillac, with a steering wheel to be envied and beautiful suspended seats above the axle, was free of any damage. The keys were on a nail inside the garage where Bess had always put them. Nan and Kate both had driven it since country children all drive, if not tractors, at least motor cars to be ready for an emergency. The car had been left to Tom by a prosperous landowner, a convert of Tom's, by way of showing gratitude. The preacher had located and, with clever persuasion, had the convert's only son released from a jail in Oklahoma. The young lawbreaker, after leaving home at an early age and not finishing secondary school, had fallen in with low-life thieves. Tom was successful in taking responsibility for the boy by convincing the sheriff he would guide the boy home again to his father's land. The red car was delivered to Mr. Heath by the same former jailbird in accordance with his father's will, but Tom immediately rejected the gift. How could a preacher accept and move around in a red Cadillac, even if it was then ten years old in 1916? But Bess's words had convinced him to take the car.

"Don't accept the attention-getting automobile for yourself, Tom. It is wild and red, like the wife you chose. My hair is red and the part of me that is free is a part that you love. Mr. Ford may persist in making his black automobiles like every car in town! This car is me and my spirit. It isn't new but I love it and you do know how to make it run forever!"

She got the car. The early model had no permanent top so that Bess's hair blew in the wind in a free and fast style she loved. The town understood. Bess could avoid reminding Tom that his only income from preaching was through contributions from his followers so that without her job at the post office and his occasional surveying work their family would be hard-up.

Also in the garage were four bicycles, the precedents for automobiles and one of the causes, along with need for efficient cross-continental mail delivery, for roads developing beyond Indian trails. Cycling protesters had made much fuss for the freedom to see the whole country westward. On any Sunday after church, barring snow or ice, the Heath foursome would be found cycling, even with occasional rests when Nan would suffer breathing difficulties from asthma.

Nan rubbed each bike clean of any mud until all looked new ... like the day Grandfather Quinn brought them to the Heath home and Otis had lined them up at the front door. Everyone in town knew of Ted's love of bicycles. He made it known that any family of his would be strong-legged bikers because he had been a champion in marathons.

On this day of searching, Nan's tears seemed unending as she said to Ned, "Let's ride away ... let's go until our legs won't move any longer ... is there a place I might reach where my family is still living?"

Ned rode with her for an hour, giving him time to build courage upon returning to the Heath property to say, "I'm alone and you're alone. Nan ... why don't you marry me? I told you before I would always take care of you ... it's no good to be by yourself ... we could be a family."

She stared at him and made no reply. Her eyes expressed bewilderment, then fury, and finally detachment. Ned backed away from her. Did she feel guilt for being away too long that night her family was consumed by smoke? He had never asked but felt sure the demons of fate, the thieves of choices in life, must have seized her heart with anguish ... what if they had never ventured out? What if they had returned much earlier? Finality seemed to him the cruelest of all realities. He would never mention his dread of her anger.

"Come with me to the fields of my grandfather's farm ... it's a nice walk and I need to gather rabbit tobacco for stuffing my pillow. My mother took Otis's advice about this ... it helps me breathe when I have an asthma attack."

The two found the fields a blending of burnt umber and patches of yellow ochre, since the corn had been harvested. Stubs would soon be snowy white or ice-covered, evenly spaced knobs, in rows before one reached erratically emerging woods, then more open fields where the rabbit tobacco grew. Four hands reached to the bottom of slender three-foot-high stalks, stripping the curly dried and crunchy leaves they sought after. Indians had smoked it for centuries, and once Nan and Kate had sneaked into fields with newspapers to roll it, and matches to light them, only to become so dizzy they had to lie looking at the sky for what seemed an eternity before standing with balance. The aroma from the plant was pungent but Nan was accustomed to it.

For two weeks, with rakes and sifting items, they found papers, pictures, clothing, and all objects except iron objects reduced near to ashes. Lazy and unemployed, except for odd jobs around the town, Mr. Wilkins could be seen peering at the two searchers. They both felt he was creepy whether he was drunk or sober. Nan's parents had expressed sympathy for this poor soul who had lost his way. They felt his family had been dealt a poor hand in this life.

Into the third week of the search the youthful figures

picked the lock on the very private workshop attached to the garage. Fire had not touched this little building. Not even Bess Heath ever visited the workshop. Tom had claimed it as his sanctuary. Nan had every right ... even obligation ... to enter and examine all properties her parents left. Still, her entry was on silent tiptoes as she whispered a plea for absolution from her father.

The small building's entire interior, walls, ceiling and wooden floors, was white-washed, so that light entering clear-story windows on three sides bounced around, enhancing the luminosity of all forms. This day was sunny. Nan understood now why Tom spent time here on sunny days and seldom on dark or rainy days; this space reflected brilliant highlights, visions of contrasts in visual values. The preacher had written his sermons here at a desk, also painted white ... a plethora of white pages with notes was scattered over the desk and floor ... but the first imports of delivery for intruders were huge drawings of nudes tacked to the walls under the high windows. The drawings recalled classical works in the library which had been peeped at by every teen since the library had obtained the art section ... drawings which were banned from the schools by minds still enslaved to Puritanism ... a mindset which, until the 1960s, in higher education fine arts classes in the United States, would demand that male models wear a jock strap while female models could pose fully nude.

Tom Heath's name was signed modestly on the bottom right corner and dated. Nan stood frozen as she studied each of the vine charcoal works, and others in red conte crayon ... she touched one but nothing smeared ... the room smelled of resin ... and turpentine ... her thoughts repeated over and over.

"No one knew! Father regularly spent time in the museum and academy in Kansas City ... but we thought he was only an appreciator! Did my mother know? Is this why she protected his privacy so? High windows, long slivers, were, of course so no one could see in ... this whole rich life!!" She understood that local citizens would think the works were indecent. The secret must be kept.

A sign above a closet door read LET ME WORK WITH HUMILITY ... THE CHALLENGE FOR SPIRITUAL GROWTH: TO WORK WITH PASSION THROUGH TALENTS BY LETTING PRIDE AND SELF-LOVE GO OUT OF ME AND INTO THE WORK.

Ned remained silent. He wanted to tell her that she had received an inheritance of utmost surprise and lasting richness.

Nan opened the unlocked closet door. Shelves, from floor to ceiling, held dozens of sketches and journals. She opened a small sketch book and read.

"'On Asymmetry and the Occult.' We'll read them together if it takes a lifetime, Ned."

The boy's rapid pulse was felt up his neck into his throbbing temples ... these were the first words which suggested she would be with him always.

"Listen to this, Ned." Nan read a few lines from a journal as if closing it would be like letting go or closing the coffin on her father.

"Opposites are not a continuum with ends but one reality folding always back on itself. Plato misjudged the poet and musician when banning them from his ideal state because of overstimulation of the arts to emotions, crippling rational thought. However, the arts are at once both sense and idea inseparably! Mozart knew this better than anyone."

"Maybe you can help me understand his words, Ned ... you are smarter than I," she murmured, replacing the pages on a shelf.

Examining the outside of the workshop before leaving

on the day of the great discovery, the two friends discovered a rotten and broken short ladder in the alley. Agitated and suspicious of any intruder. Ned examined the clapboard under the high windows. Finding no sign of paint damage made Nan confident that the wondrous works inside had not been seen.

4
Ned's Agenda

Ralph Hahn's folks had practically founded the town, having been one of the first farming families in the Midwest when land was a territory, not a state, when no one associated large acreage with much more than the right to work hard, survive, and leave offspring well-positioned to stay. In addition to farming, and raising dairy cows, Ralph's father had, some years back, also become the town's mortician, using one of the numerous out-buildings for burial preparations, eventually turning a larger barn into part-carriage house and part-morgue. It was common for early settlers to take on a business after having to learn to do something no one else could do at a time of crisis. Ralph's father had prepared a family member's body for burial and then did the same for neighbors, determining him to be a mortician; a local pharmacist pulled a tooth once and then was known as the "dentist." A Hahn hayloft was turned into a facility to house hired men who helped with both farm and funeral work. The spread of land was enviable, a thousand acres reaching across a wide and deep property, meant for a crew of sons to work. But several daughters came to the Hahns before the last child, a son, Ralph. History then repeated itself, giving Ralph and his wife five girls! Through two generations, the Hahns relied on hired help to keep the farm running until daughters married, bringing husbands to work on their land.

When Ned rode into town, two years prior to the Heath fire, on a fine smoky white mare unlike the heavier work horses, mules and asses used by farmers, it seemed a destined vacuum for him to fill for Ralph Hahn. Tall and underfed at sixteen, he quickly convinced Mr. Hahn of his qualities to learn fast and work hard, both at farm and funeral duties. Later, fast-failing victims of the so-called Spanish flu epidemic, when one out of every five Americans fell ill to it, proved Ned's abilities to be a blessing to Mr. Hahn. The town knew of the Hahns' attachment to the boy who would be suspect by locals except for his candid tale of having run away from a drunken father and harsh beatings, his great love for his mother, and his intention to return to her when he could make his way. Besides, he was lanky, with beautiful facial bone structure, topped with thick chestnut hair. The brightness of his blue eyes was captivating, especially since he had the gift of turning a phrase to suit even the smallest encounter with the elderly women or the school master. He was lighthearted, and to be in his company created endorphins in any brain.

With a job secured Ned was admitted into the high school halfway into the school year. Strangers were slow to be accepted by both young and old but Ned, having been the youngest of five brothers, was adept at both football and baseball. Some of the beatings he suffered from his father came when he took time off from work in the cornfields to play. The boy spoke in a more refined manner and in proper English. He explained, so as to not appear snobbish, that his mother had spoken a bit differently from farm folks because she had been sent to a school as a teenager where speech was stressed. It had separated her somewhat from the farm folks. Mr. Hahn, having no sons, and loving sports, worked out a schedule so that Ned could participate in the games. Ned did it well. Girls noticed him. The guys accepted him. But even beyond that, when he proved to be a sharp poker player, ride the fastest horse, and crack and swallow a dozen raw eggs when lingering on a street corner at dusk with the guys, he won the admiration he needed to be comfortable in the community.

One occasion had presented itself as an interruption to acceptance. Ned's brother, Colby, appeared in Flat Rock in the second year of Ned's settling there to tell Ned that James, an older brother, had been killed in a foxhole somewhere in France called Belleau Wood, where the American doughboys had defeated the Germans in a battle. A Red Cross ambulance had delivered the wounded Cane to one of the overseas base hospitals where he died. This older brother had signed up to fight for America as soon as Wilson and the Congress created the elective Service system in 1917, mandating that all males twenty-one to thirty register. When a few items came to the Cane farm in Oklahoma Ned's name was taped to a wristwatch. The timepiece was gold with a gold chain band unlike anything the Canes had ever seen. For fear it might be sold, and feeling determined the rightful beneficiary have the watch, Colby set out to find Ned.

"How did you find me?" asked Ned.

"Your friend Jake, the Indian, knew where you were. Don't be surprised if he comes to see you."

The brothers had never been close but the younger boy admired Colby's strength and his stature, which was burly and much taller than most men. His wild streak had him on the run, having stolen horses to drive down to Tucson, Arizona where news had it that the first municipal airport was being built. He planned to sell the horses, find Ned, head for Tucson, and learn to fly. Indians bought the horses before he crossed the line into Kansas. His passion for aviation was not new. As the brothers visited late into the evening, they shared belly laughs as they relived stories of how each of the five

Cane brothers had dreamed of adventures. Early in the war a news item reported how five aviators dropped a hundred dead bombs for practice in Hempstead Plains, New York, but none of them landed within thirty feet of the targets, which were twenty feet in diameter. That same week, in Central Park in Manhattan, aviators were giving flights to passengers who brought certificates to support the war. This winged patriotism became Colby's goal in his inmost soul for himself. When the war ended, his passion for learning to fly did not subside.

Will Cane's magnetic force was simply the road and opening trails. With the Federal Road Act of 1916, meant to promote general welfare by connecting states and better regulate commerce, Will, the oldest of the brothers, took off to get a job with the Auto Association of America by painting telegraph poles on the "Trail to Sunset" from Kansas City towards Santa Fe, and on to Los Angeles, or wherever the hell they took him. It was eventually south to the Mexican state of Chihuahua.

Perry Cane was a mama's boy who hung around the farm, taking abuse longer than the others and continuing his first love, fishing. He was not as bright as the others, but could fix any machine of any type and was never without a girl by his side.

Upon Colby's departure from Flat Rock, Ned returned to his school schedule wearing the wrist watch. Having never seen such a thing, all the students stared at the fancy "jewelry," leading the boys to begin calling him fancy-pants and accusing him of wearing a woman's bracelet … and further, calling him a queer. There was nothing to do then but beat up a couple of the big guys with whom he played football, then stand off all the others while explaining that his brother and all the doughboys in France were wearing this thing in the war because turning a wrist in a fight of heavy gunfire is easier than reaching and digging for a pocket watch. His brother died with it on his wrist.

"I'll kill anyone who utters a word of insult to his memory ... none of y'awl have ever been out of this hick one-horse town, or Kansas, and wouldn't know what's going on in the world. This isn't the last time I'll be attacked by ignorant dumb-asses."

A gush of tears and unrelenting trembling came over the boy ... he realized he hadn't cried over James's death ... he hadn't cried since running away from home ... and now he fell deeper into sobs, fed by earliest impressions of his father's keeping him on constant guard against eruptions of bombastic explosions of fury. He could still hear the roaring of the large brawny man which sent all five sons, Ned the youngest, hightailing out of reach of the mighty and powerful fists. James was always the fastest on his feet. To a small boy nothing could match the fear and terror he felt when the drink brought those fists to his mother's body. Was he weeping over the death of James ... for the terrified brothers as they fled in fear from the father ... or from homesickness for his mother he longed to see? He would wear the watch every day for the rest of his long life.

Schoolmates scattered quickly to leave Ned in his grief. That was the last battle for acceptance. Young people in the town began to admire the watch and consider that a wrist watch might be a worldly fashion.

With these hard-won social victories, he quietly observed the only female in the high school with whom he was smitten. Nan Heath was quiet and serious about her studies, liked by the girls, admired by the boys, but stood somewhat apart. Some said it was because of the strictness of her father, a Mormon minister. Others said she was quiet because, if over-excited, she was known to have asthmatic seizures. Ned would wait, and cautiously approach this prize when he could plan a strategy. His loneliness set his imagination afire with plans which granted no lingering in the hallways of his mind, but moved to a lighted atrium of actions. His goal was to call on Nan, although no other young men had been granted that privilege. His designs for gaining entry into Nan's life demanded patience and acquisition of information. He learned the preacher's sympathies and interests. Mr. Heath loved horses, automobiles, and the Mormon Church. Ned had the horse and horse knowledge, was capable enough at working under the hoods of automobiles because his four older brothers had tinkered with all sorts of farm equipment and machines, and the research on Mormons was available in the library. Ned had, in his young life, suffered a tragic loss connected with Mormons. His brother, Will Cane, had left the farm several years prior to Ned's running away, hoping to find work on the Trail to Sunset continuing out of Kansas City on to Santa Fe and Albuquerque, but had failed to be hired. He had continued on to Rio Grande where he was persuaded to work with Mormon miners in Chihuahua, Mexico. Mexicans massacred the working crews as they emerged from mines on an evening when word passed through Chihuahua that President Wilson and the Mexican government were enemies over trade and Wilson had given material support to Huerta's opposition. Will was killed with the Mormons. Could Ned relate this story for sympathy from the preacher? He did.

Pamphlets and instructions on new automobile mechanics and the Mormon Church began to arrive in the mail addressed to Ned at Hahn's Mortuary. Thus began a year's endeavor to win favor. He learned that Mormons had left New York State because of resentment shown to them, followed by threats of bodily harm, and eventually to property burnings. After moving west to Pennsylvania a Mormon church at

Buck Valley was destroyed by dynamite. With sincerity, the boy with a big agenda felt the evil of hate, the same hate he had seen shown to his Indian friends in Oklahoma, and the more guarded hate for the Quinns, he heard, for their "Romish" beliefs. Ned's knowledge of the Mormon Church, his intelligence and skills with engines, and his willingness to get under the hoods of cars were qualities which led Tom Heath and Ned into many a conversation and advancement in the younger man's design to visit the Heath's home. Ned was most delighted when he could offer any bit of information to the preacher.

Once when he had ridden Mollie to the Heath house Tom admired the shine of the mare's coat and quizzed Ned as to how he got it so glossy. Ned answered coolly, "I always gave my parent's horses raw eggs to eat, which the horses, if loose, would steal from the hen house anyway if given a chance, because I knew, from an Indian friend of mine, it would make their manes, tails, and overall coats glisten."

They worked together and ate together when Bess Heath would invite Ned to dinner. She understood his secret heart when no one else did. How could anyone miss it when, sitting so near to Nan around a dining table, his face would seem a Franz Hals portrait, comically red-cheeked.

5

A Union

A justice of the peace married Nan and Ned in the Hahn's big house. Most of the people attending had been at the burial. Ella paid for refreshments and presented the couple with a generous envelope containing enough cash to hold them over for the approaching winter season and beyond into spring. Otis and Sadie came to promise the couple a home-baked pie each week, especially the local favorite, gooseberry, when in season. Ella had even given Nan a wedding street-length dress and shoes to match, which surprised the town because although Ella paid what she owed quickly she was most parsimonious when it came to gifting. She and her friend Cora had rushed into Kansas City to fetch the outfit, to present themselves as generous, but mostly to preserve Ella's false pride by avoiding the bride's showing up in grungy clothes. She presented Ned with an expensive wide silk tie with the Saks trademark, and, knowing little of style herself, counted on Cora to pick out the very posh high-button shoes for the bride. Still, the aunt failed to host the ceremony in her own fine farm house. Everything there at the Quinn place, since her folks' death three years earlier, seemed closed off and anyone entering an intruder.

Ella quizzed Ralph Hahn about a proper suit for Ned, but Ralph had already arranged for one of his sons-in-law, who happened to be Ned's size, to offer the groom a proper suit. A fancy shawl was presented to Nan by Mrs. Hahn. The girl remembered her mother's pointing out this same wrap to her husband when she had seen it in *Ladies' Home Journal* in the summer, with hopes he might take the hint and order it for her Christmas present. Whenever the new bride wore it, she imagined her mother's loving the ethereal lightness of silk.

Being shaken by her family's recent deaths, and with exaggerated fear of the coldness of burials, both symbolically and physically, the irony of living in these digs ... Ned's small furnished room with a walk-down toilet and pull-chain shower ... was not lost on Nan, and was the safe walls she needed, but a wood-burning stove gave the two a secure space for evenings. Nan had no need to enter the preparation rooms below, where Ned would assist in preparing the dead for interment. There, in early mornings, a joy in learning and studying together developed while eating Ned's cooking.

In the evenings of that extended mourning period, adorned with the Thanksgiving, Christmas and Easter seasons, Nan studied, with Ned's help. She had been removed from school because of her marital status. The boy's quick mind had sailed him through the same academics the year before, making him the perfect support for her studies. With energetic wit, his language was full of unusual quips by which he could toss an image like a clown juggling for an audience, and take a bow when folks obviously admired his imagination. Work, food, and daily routines seemed easy enough, but sharing the marriage bed was awkward to both. The two lived chastely and modestly for weeks above the mortuary neither being threatened by the other's aggressiveness. Both were virgins. They were friends.

A singular occasion had given Nan the greatest pleasure and greatest terror simultaneously. There had been a third-birthday party for her, and at the end of a happy day the small girl lay, tired and warm, snuggled in the "Baby Bed" with slats, which she refused to give up yet. Her little fingers explored herself. A tiny thumb moved gently back and forth between her legs on a warm spot, back and forth, back and forth and a thrill rushed from the spot through her entire little body throbbing again and again. What pleasure! What a great secret!!! But into the dark room, a figure entered to tuck her in. Her mother took the small hand, and leaning down whispered, "You must never touch that … the Bad man will get you when you die. The Bad Man is the Devil." As thrilling as the orgasm just experienced had been, the terror which seized her, as she lay shaking, hit with even greater force, not from fears of any devil but from the first conscious awareness of her immortality, the first realization that parents could not protect her from Death. Before, at the deaths of her baby chicks, Spot the collie dog and her neighbor's cat, Nan had been blind to inclusion of herself in dying, unaware that all time moved toward her inevitable end. This would not be forgiven. Never. The two first Loves … love objects … Mother and Father, would fail and fall themselves, helpless to protect her from this thing called dying. Terror persisted nightly with orgasms a solitary relief. Asthmatic seizures began soon after that night, following a bee sting on her finger. Although Nan remained a strong child overall, and was content to live in her dreamworld, most contacts with others were simply an interruption. Asthmatic infectious bronchitis was a regular visitor by age five so that her constant companion was a glass atomizer with small rubber squeezer attached. A liquid adrenalin spray, inhaled through her mouth by squeezing the rubber ball attached to the atomizer, would relieve her so that the suffocating panic seizures of closed bronchial tubes would pass. She had named this lifesaver Agnes … Agnes Atomizer. She even slept with it under her pillow, indebted to the traveling doctor who knew of the medication and had informed Tom and Bess of two chemists' success in separating this hormone before Nan was even born. The little girl would use it whenever needed, but adults needed to be cautious because this natural hormone was a powerful heart stimulant.

Nan had been a bright hope as a singer for Mr. Heath's Sunday services, but her great ear and lovely young voice became awkward and strained. All the songs of heaven and Jesus and God's mercy were memorize from Nan's earliest life along with numerous doxologies. These concepts dulled with images of the Bad man, her nightly pursuit of warmth and escape from terror. She "went to the Garden alone … when the dew was still on the roses … " but her garden of relief was in bed and secret.

And she could "come, come, come, come," not to "the little church in the wildwood" but to a "place so dear to her childhood," her nightly naughtiness. Even Ned would never be told of this. She had not connected her night pleasures with men or love-making, never having been enlightened by her mother. Since no one ever mentioned the experience of throbbing thrills, the seventeen-year-old was happy to lie down and simply snuggle with her husband, pleasing herself during morning showers. Ned's innocent touching was healing and the intimacy so intense she never thought of separation from the sweet boy who loved her.

6

Parents

Both of Nan's parents were considered highly educated for the times. As postmistress, Bess Heath knew, or had connected in some way, with nearly everyone in the county, including the county superintendent of schools. Dr. Page on hearing of the newly orphaned Nan Heath, sent instructions for Nan to be given tests regularly in the spring term to enable her to finish high school. Nan took the initiative herself to find a tutor although her husband's guidance was her true support. She decided to ask her aunt for help.

Here was the rub. Ella Quinn had not spoken to her sister Bess more than a couple of times a year for as long as Nan could remember. The Quinn homestead was deeded to Ella when Bess married the Mormon. The house was one of the largest in the town, and much more than was needed by an unmarried woman. Nan could not remember being in her grandparents' home except for their double funeral when she was fourteen and Katie was nine.

On the eve of big holidays, the graying couple would drive to the Heath place and honk their automobile horn, expecting the two grandchildren to scramble out to join them. They did with eagerness, perhaps because the older couple was unlike anyone they knew or perhaps because these kinfolks were jollier than other people. But most likely because these two touched, and kissed, and pinched each other openly in a way that embarrassed whomever they encountered. This

Sunday Rides

made the girls giggle, and feel happier on these rare days than they ever felt in the Heath house. Sometimes they were taken into the city, sometimes just into the countryside for a picnic. In Ted Quinn's Maxwell HB Touring Car, with two cylinders and twenty horsepower, the foursome took rides, as did many families from Nebraska and Kansas, on Sundays, across the prairies and off the roads and trails, with open air taking their breaths as they bumped along, with the suspended fenders having been spit-shined before their gay spin. Besides, the Quinns' car would go up to thirty-five miles an hour and was a lustrous cream color with brass lanterns on both sides of the windshield, along with large grand headlights. This grandfather did not hide his pride in the 1907 Maxwell, a high step above the more commonly bought and lower-priced Model T Fords. In 1909, when Ralph Hahn bought a Ford Model T with four cylinders and twenty-twenty-two horsepower and could run away from Ted at forty-five miles an hour, Ted ordered a Moline touring car with four vertical cylinders, a three-speed transmission and thirty-five horsepower, which would go up to fifty miles an hour! For the Quinns, any approaching car on those prairie drive days was a challenge to race. Ted and his bride would drive that Moline off the river bridge in 1916 to their deaths. The Maxwell remained in the Quinns' barn. The sisters always regretted parting from the lovers.

The big family break occurred before Bess and Tom's marriage. Having managed to emotionally recover from the announcement by their younger daughter that she would marry outside her faith, the older couple invited Tom to their farmhouse to discuss marriage plans. The two men, both with chips on their shoulders, stood with auras of energy hot enough to give physicists a heyday for imaging electrical forces from each masculine silhouette exchanging firings as if at war.

All this before the talk began.

Bess and Tom first met in the post office where, soon after Tom bought a small house in Flat Rock, he came to ask for a mailbox. The attraction was immediate. She traveled with him on Sundays when he served as minister to folks in surrounding communities who were of the Mormon faith. Now, on this late spring Sunday evening, Tom's simple Suffolk-style wagon, all of ash with seats for two, meant for travel and hauling, turned off the town road onto the half-mile drive up to the Quinns' home, the contrast in Tom's finances and Bess's parents' money shouted out through Mr. Quinn's brougham parked near the front veranda, a covered carriage of fine ironwork and carpentry, elegant upholstery, and a paint finish like glass. Although not a severe contrast between opulence and poverty, these symbols of transport made Tom uncomfortable.

The first few moments seemed pleasant enough as Sadie served lemonade in crystal glasses with Southern cheese straws on silver trays. This style was extraordinary to a country family at this time, but very much a part of Ted's and Lizzy's past in the East. The future groom had agreed to marry in the church of the bride's choice, not understanding that he must become Catholic, and raise all Heath children as Roman Catholics.

"Did you know that I am a Mormon minister? You and I are both Christians. With mutual honoring we could make Bess happy. She looks for harmony. Her original family is dear to her, hence please allow our union to be as blessed with serenity as yours and Mrs. Quinn's has been. I can't change my religion any more than you could. I will never have my children worship away from my own calling," Tom strained in delivery.

36

Lizzy Quinn, regretting her husband's confrontation so early in this meeting, turned white and stared at Bess as Ella joined them. Lizzy feared the worst … that the soon-to-be bride would not side with her parents but might be severed from closeness with them.

The fiery blue eyes of the Irishman were registering rage.

"Well, before we continue, my good man, let us move beyond this fruit drink of the ladies and have a belt of scotch!"

"I do not partake of the stuff and will forbid my wife and any children of ours to do so … their bodies and minds would be modified from clean … but I accept your habits or weaknesses, whichever." Tom knew that Bess had informed her father of his stand on this matter.

"I can assure you that Mrs. Quinn and I are indeed clean, and perhaps your particular Bible had left out the part that Christ drank wine with his disciples … do you bend to grape juices or does your faith ignore our Lord's communion? I understand you do not approve of coffee. Is that true? And where is the fun in your life? There are great rules, like great religions for living, but humans are meant to play and love! Bare bones and starkness, without celebrations which humans need through the great arts of the Florentine flavor in life, leave life too dreary. Your protestors were led by an angry Catholic monk in attempts to strip our faith of celebrations."

The Mormon replied before the words were clearly out of Quinn's mouth. "Yes, Luther was angered by the ostentatious riches of your church leaders and the mendacious pope who, after squandering the church treasure, and owing every big bank in Rome, sold pieces of paper to peasants promising them entry into heaven so he could refill his chest of riches. Shame … shame on this history! And, sir, we do know how to play, and even allow our leaders to love a woman, which is the great experience a man is granted by God!"

For the first time in Ella's life, she was looking at her

father pausing in an argument. Tom continued in Ted's hesitation.

"As for the bread and blood, we are able, as men in a democracy with individual consciences, to adopt rituals of more modern and appropriate particulars. As one who lives in ambiguity of a free land of democracy yet under a one-man authority of your Pope, you will not understand our more open thought."

Ted was ready now.

"Yes, open ... open enough to take as many wives to bed with you as you like, and how can you deny this is pagan? I will never agree to your marrying my girl without your converting to our faith ... and only one wife!"

"I do not believe in polygamy, sir. It is outlawed in my church today. There was a time when traveling communities would suffer the deaths of men and husbands, leaving wives without any support ... or promise of children. I do not believe in this myself ... but women are still considered chattels, and unable to own property ... many a spinster has had to turn to the streets in cities ... what is worse? I know the depth of my love for Bess will allow me nothing except pure love and loyalty to her ... we do not sin easily, do not accept absolution through a middle-man, but go with our bare bones to God for forgiveness."

There could be no return to pleasantries of conversing, as Ted responded.

"This is a revelation that you are of an alien temperament to my family and will never be blessed to marry Bess! You Protestants may cry democracy while Mormons simply proclaim Divine appointment of your leader who rules, unquestioned, to speak for God. Where is your individual conscience? Your history is shallow and demands deeper study of books beyond frontier hearsay! You are not welcome here. Leave our land and my daughter's side!"

Bess left with him. Both men nurtured the severance, by silently avoiding each other and by closing their minds to ever becoming family to each other. Until both of their deaths they remained at loggerheads, denying any possibility of healing the rift.

7

Grandparents

From colonial times Baltimore had been the home of the majority of Roman Catholics in America, who received constant and often dangerous threats from Protestants when living elsewhere. The spiritual guidance for the Catholic Church was given by Jesuits, meeting, as bishops did, several times in the first half of the nineteenth century, in Baltimore. By 1890, the largest number of immigrants being of the Catholic faith, determined this religion to be the largest in the country.

Reaction to this growth stirred the Nativist Movement to vilify Catholics in sensational newspaper stories questioning the patriotism of the "Romish." Bloody riots were set off in Philadelphia leaving even greater hatred between the Protestants and Catholics.

John Quinn, when the nineteenth century was well past its midpoint, feeling the security of a city with many of his religion and knowing that in frontiers and small communities his beliefs would not be accepted, settled in Baltimore and married Mary Kelley, daughter of wealthy Bostonian importers. John and Mary were blessed with comforts and three children, the oldest of them Ted. The boy was, by school age, a tough kid, quick to use his fists in the city streets. He and his two younger sisters were playful, with quick wits on the cuff of their sleeves.

The redheaded, stocky boy was sent to church school

and then placed in seminary training in hopes of quelling his feistiness to spark with authorities. Mary Quinn argued that if Ted did choose the priesthood as his life's work there would be no more Quinn line. This comment brought laughter to John who was convinced his son would never be self-disciplined enough to reach being ordained. Perhaps to spite his father Ted did make that ceremony in full commitment as he threw himself on the cathedral floor before the altar for final vows. His unorthodox manner and frivolous style delivered him as a somewhat shocking young priest to parishioners not appreciating that a Father might be high-spirited as well as fun-loving. He had annoyed many in the church leadership by saying, "When my priesthood ceases to be fun I shall leave."

And so play he did, at his vocation, while for a decade he was also first to rise for duties, saying more masses and visiting more sick ... even holding the record of more conversions ... than any priest in Baltimore. He was beguiling.

His own escapes were through entering himself in bicycling marathons. Secretly! Of course this would not be condoned by his superiors. His dream was to enter the marathon in New York City's Madison Square Garden, but decided to save that venture. He begged for a retreat to Boston where he entered a most competitive event of cycling, not visiting his relatives since both of his mother's parents had died, but going straight to learn entry procedures and view the large tent covering the racing oval. The raceway seemed much too soft, and not having his own cycle left him at a disadvantage. Since money was not an issue because of his mother's wealth, which clandestinely reached Ted in spite of his vows of poverty. Ted rented the cycle best designed for least wind resistance. Cyclists were challenged to a six-day ride ... round and round and round, with only necessary stops for body urgencies, resting and brief dozes. The first to finish the required laps in six days would win. The Irishman, shedding clerical garb, free of the collar, won the marathon! This only spurred him on to enter more of these endurance tests. The contests had to run shorter periods since occasional time off from priestly duties might only allow a two-or three-day endurance test cycling. He was clever at avoiding any news photos when receiving the trophy and registered under a false name so that his family and church authorities would not know of the private indulgence. He entered other marathons and was consistently victorious.

The young priest's transfer to a Savannah church came as an alarm to Mary Quinn. She had managed to see her son, the joy of her heart, regularly because, being a very generous donor to the church, she was allowed to fetch her son's laundry each week and return it pressed beyond the ordinary requirements, but also smelling of great seasonings. She would sneak a baked chicken, some raw steaks and sweets in among the cassocks. His vows of poverty would be playfully adulterated then, but eventually completely obliterated.

Ted, for once, was spontaneously obedient in accepting the transfer. His heart longed for new vistas, and adventures. Besides, a ten-year reunion for his graduating class from seminary to ordination was to be convened in Savannah. He was eager to see his old friends. Within a few weeks after assuming his new duties in the Southern city his classmates arrived at the hosting-church, not displaying a great increase in grey hair, but a noticeable decrease in spiritual energy and soaring laughter which Ted fondly associated with their time leading to ordinations. Exciting ideas were absent as the priest seemed to be feeling the undertow of time and pressures from above, along with submission to feelings of entrapment in celibacy as they gave up resistance to a leaden weight ... gravity's pull to subservience. It was easier to give in for most.

But during this reunion Ted realized that the noble path he had chosen was the wrong one for him. It had taken ten years of asking himself who he was, and what he truly wanted to be, before the uneasiness of total obedience, which often seemed to deny him individual consciousness as well as a search for ideals not found in dogmas, began to strangle him. In the days following the reunion Ted felt a paralysis of devotion to his duties. Feelings of being chewed up suffocated him with sorrow. A final decision to make a move came through sudden grieving when his mother suffered a fatal heart attack. Still, his courage was puny, disallowing a surge of putting things in place by approaching his family, his good friends, and his superiors.

During his service in Savannah Ted had regularly, with serious focus, acted as confessor for nuns. Their convent was part of the church where he resided and where he prepared diligently for the nuns each week. Years later he would wish that he had kept notes on these confessions to a fairly inexperienced priest. He had yearned desperately to have these spiritual women open up to him through a mystical and spiritual response, but found that a more realistic attitude to the sacrament and to their disciplines enabled them to say what was truly breaking their hearts, what was agonizingly experienced as loneliness, frustration and shocking dismay in attempting to be religious. The superhuman job for him was to not just listen, or pray for them, but to somehow give them strength in solutions to day by day problems.

Lizzy Seltzer, a novice in the convent, sought him out for confessions. When he first looked at her face his heart jumped in his throat. It was then the training concept of "custody of the eyes," of avoiding looking at any subject which was overstimulating to physical responses or thoughts, became a giant challenge. As a priest, he had made jokes with other seminarians about harnessing his eyes to minimize any excitation to sexual temptations. He had been successful in following the rules until Lizzy's face enchanted him. He found it impossible to avoid her eyes as they greeted each other, and as they took their leave his eyes would follow her as he fantasized how her soft young face would feel to his touch. He already knew the smell of her freshly pressed habit as well as her long girlish fingers ... underneath the very full and flowing black garments must be long and slender arms and legs. She seemed almost as tall as he. Her confessions were so simple and so innocent ... but candid concerning her doubts.

On a hot, deep southern July day, not far from the cotton exchange and near the river, the young man caught sight of the redheaded priest ... but then again how could this be? The muscular Irishman could not be her priest because he was not in clerical dress. She looked again at the shock of red wavy hair and laughing eyes as the man disappeared into a large tent for a cycling marathon. She and several nuns had become aware that Savannah was holding such a contest through posters tacked to gas lights along the many square parks in the city, through which they were allowed to stroll when delivering gifts to the poor and the sick. Each day of the marathon Lizzy would manage to peep in to the marathon tent to see whether her vision was in fact true. It was. Father Quinn was in the competition. Father Quinn also won, she later learned through the newspapers. This time he did not escape photographers as he received the trophy! Was it fate that brought down the wrath of church leaders in Savannah who notified the Bishop of Baltimore of this disgraceful behavior? There was always gambling around the races and drinking, with wild parties. Was it Ted's unconscious need to be found out? Was it the need to hold Lizzy's face in his hands and to speak of his suffocating struggles to be obedient?

John Quinn had lost a wife, and now, through humiliation for himself and his daughters, disowned his son, directing Ted to leave their home. Application for dispensation to Rome was out of the question ... no bishop would recommend an appeal to the Holy See that this priest be released from vows. He would be denied any privileges in the church, and, although not important enough to be a person excommunicated, he would be banished from any priestly life. He could only repeat to himself for the rest of his life,

"Once a priest, always a priest ... I love my Church."

Ted left with assurance from lawyers that his inheritance from his mother would be mailed to him as long as he lived if he did not return to Baltimore. Any last will and testament of his would be honored by the family's executors of estates. He left, and left with Lizzy. They both knew that a great and passionate love was already filling their hearts. They also knew a move to the West would require that they keep private the fact that their monies were from an inheritance well beyond even the average successful American businessman's at the latter part of the nineteenth century. They had their love, their health, and wealth to start an adventure towards the great frontier from which they would never return.

Flat Rock would never know the whole story of Ted and Lizzy Quinn. They came from the East with secrets and kept them. They could not, and would not, hide the fact that Ted was rich man ... that income came through a Kansas City bank regularly, and that the Quinns were Catholics and generous.

How could Ted repeat his father's choosing religious rules over a child? John Quinn's banishment of his son was parodied by that son when Bess was not forgiven for marrying a Mormon. Was this radical attitude born of enslavement to tenets? Was it a fatal uncoiling of obedience to the true master-with-whip-in-hand, coercing all actions: ego? Did pride kindle all actions? Pride, fear of death, guilt, ambition, on the final slate ... ego, or lack of it, wins.

45

8

Explorations and Love

Although Ned was Nan's true support for learning, knowing that her aunt Ella was smart, and was warming up to her, Nan ventured to the Quinn place in hopes of getting Ella to tutor her through tests towards graduation. Having spent some special outings with Ella's parents, the grandparents, Nan was curious about the Quinn property, knowing that although Ted Quinn wanted to be generous with his granddaughters and that Tom Heath would not have it, Nan always felt like the poor relatives, which they were. Ella, as far as Bess knew, had inherited everything; the land, house, and the much-gossiped-about fortune. The spinster did not decline the tutoring proposition, but reluctantly agreed, placing strict parameters on her time. The girl was to come early in the morning, twice a week. This would allow Nan to be on her way with little bother to Ella.

There was a boarder in the house, a shopkeeper with very opposite presence to Ella's. Cora Andrews seemed to have a permanent smile and unending supply of alacrity in spite of a recent gloomy past. The flu epidemic had taken her husband and only son, but after a brief grieving period, she bounced back, running her clothing shop three months after the burials. Jack Andrews had been the town joke, liked by everyone, a dreamer with winning ways, but without a bone of seriousness or strength for raising a family. He might show up for his clerking job in the town's largest general store, or he might just take off to fish or cycle around the countryside. Bills were seldom paid in full or on time. Cora had married her high school sweetheart when she was hyper-sexually driven, and, in the heat of his teens, Jack was her match. This otherwise seemingly shy duo was inseparable. Without Cora's early interest and involvement in the Women's Party in Kansas City, which led her to read all the printed material she could get her hands on about feminine issues, including Sanger's methods for prevention of childbirth, printed as early as 1914 out of New York ... without these interests Jack and Cora would have had a half-dozen kids before they were twenty-one. Cora's interest in birth control emerged from early tragedies. She was the only surviving child born to her mother, who had given birth to four other babies born dead, the last one taking the life of the mother. As it was, the Andrews were both twenty-two before their son was born. Both before and after Cora's pregnancy, Ella Quinn came on board, as a bookkeeper, to help solve the Andrews' monetary problems.

An unflinching martinet, she assigned a budget and a strict list for what could be spent as she dealt with merchants to settle debts for the couple. Cora was advised to get a job as a saleswoman in the town's only shoe store so she could pay the family's bills. Ella then was able to get a bank loan for Cora to set up her own shop for men's, women's, and children's clothing. Finally Jack could piddle around and be accepted by his friends, seeming to have no regrets or shame in his new role, free of pressures. Cora had been loyal, but she lost interest in her husband. She was the bread winner who "wore the pants" at a time when she needed affection. Ella and Cora found each other after the loss of Cora's son and husband. The widow moved into the big house with Ella.

On an earlier-than-usual arrival to Ella's house in December Nan entered the front hallway of the large farmhouse to sense no one stirring. That is, until she heard giggling coming from one of the bedrooms upstairs and, looking up, saw Cora leave Ella's room. Nan thought how nice it must be to have such a close friend, close like sisters … until she realized that the sounds through the opened door recalled the playful breathing and laughter which she recognized as expressions of her romantic grandparents. She spoke to Ned of this realization and the wise boy responded, "Everyone gets lonely … unbearably lonely I suppose."

This close affection had not yet been shared by the young couple.

Mr. Hahn paid Ned well enough for his work, and out of pride, Ella would never have her niece go without life's necessities. Still, when an opportunity came for the couple to work at the State Asylum for the Insane and Infirmed just three miles outside Flat Rock, they accepted a position in which Ned would care for the building, and serve meals, while Nan would clean the patients' rooms and even occasionally help them bathe. The job required them to report for work three eight-hour days a week, since other state workers covered the rest of the week.

They began their work in the asylum in January when exceptionally heavy snows demanded bicycles be stored and the red Cadillac be used for transportation. Bitter cold accompanied repetitive snows so that without central heating in the institute Ned was worked to a straining point to keep logs in each fireplace and flues opened. In warmer months the grounds had been kept mowed and raked to a minimally manicured condition by a chain gang out of Kansas City. These inmates shoveled roads and paths when blizzards made access to the asylum difficult. Knowing the schedule of the chain gang's work days, Ned would insist that Nan not accompany him to the Asylum on those days for fear his beautiful wife might be too attractive to the prisoners. Doctors seemed for the most part kind enough when they visited, but their performances could fit a near no-show category.

Nan's life took a dramatic turn during this period. The turn seemed to lessen the frequency of days when Nan felt she was starting from day one in facing the deaths of her family. A beautiful teenage boy with golden locks and olive skin contrasting with his ultramarine blue eyes, had been admitted to the asylum because of epilepsy. His mother, having lost her husband to influenza, had married a man unsympathetic to the boy's condition and convinced his wife to admit Felix to the State's asylum. Nan and Ned were both charmed by the boy whose intelligence was demonstrated in games and routine duties. It seemed to the couple that he should be at home with parents and not with older patients who were mentally disturbed or retarded. Felix was only a couple of years younger than the Canes who themselves were more children than adults ... children in positions of great responsibility. The Canes made even dreary, dark days of winter cheerful. Their youth, health, and energy contrasted with the old, sick and sad. It was not a cruel comparison but a reckoning with the brightness of anticipating many new seasons and years. Work then was not resisted. This infirmary awakened them to their blessings which they discussed at the end of each day.

On an unusually warm and sunny March day, with snows melting rapidly, Felix fled from the buildings, not unnoticed by Nan. In only his tan Levi overalls, no shirt or shoes, the boy dashed out into the sunlight and ran up a tree-covered hill, a hill with closely spaced small cedars which had been chewed away by deer, leaving only the top growth full and bushy. The cedars took on humanlike standing images. Nan followed close behind Felix, urging him to return to the warmth of the buildings and avoid illness. Catching up to him she realized she could not physically drag him back. The escapee darted in and out of the cedars as Nan tried to catch him by his over-

49

alls' shoulder straps and coax him to a safer place. Fearing that Felix might have a seizure on the icy ground, and having seen a doctor take action to keep the boy from choking, she did not want to be left with the obligation of aiding him. As she decided to return to get Ned's help, Felix jumped in front of her, grabbing her around the waist, laughing heartily as she struggled to free herself. The youth whispered, "I just want to touch you," and pulled her close to him so that she felt his hard heat between her legs as he began moving himself up and down against his prisoner for only a couple of moments but long enough for Nan to lose her breath, and through her clothing gain her first ecstasy shared with another. Felix smiled, unashamed, and released her to follow her back inside.

Startled and mystified by such instantly achieved orgasm, a thrill not self-induced, Nan found her husband so that the boy could be dried and a much-needed change of clothes given to him. More than this request by her would not be uttered. It had not been the jailed men who had stepped out of line. The young wife was not angered ... not repulsed ... but rather indebted to this beautiful male she would continue to befriend as she moved on to another depth in her marriage.

To Ned's surprise. Nan snuggled up to him in bed on that cold night, searching for his mouth, letting him know that her body yearned to be held in mergence with his. Much less than this had regularly made Ned's heart beat thunderously in reaction to Nan's innocent touches, but now he felt he would truly die of the pounding in his head, his heart, and his erected organ, so gently moving now under her gown. Quick to respond, and quick to finish together, with no pain but only joy and wonder, the bed of companions was now a lovers' bed. The love-making was repeated over and over, leaving spots of blood, the tell-tale evidence of the virgin at dawn. Both partners laughed out loud and ate heartily the breakfast Ned prepared. The two laughed again as Nan walked down the stairs to shower with some obvious discomfort in her groin. Anticipation of discovering each other completely became their obsession. Over the next few weeks Nan learned of the deeper spasms of vaginal orgasms beyond the easier-targeted and shallow clitoral orgasms. She pondered whether Ted or Lizzy, or both her grandparents, had handed down to her this love of love! Sex would never grow old to either of them as they would both bring a creative spirit to bed, taking in the naturalness of every pleasure. Tragic fate put these two together. Now the other side of Janus's mask, of laughter, would be worn by the lovers.

Twin Doctors

51

Twin doctors, Gary and Glenn Muller, oversaw the health, dying, and incipience of life in Flat Rock. Having finished their studies as physicians at the University of Kansas, the young doctors took up their residence and new practice in the hometown of their mother, Mrs. Hahn's cousin, about the same time Ned Cane came to Flat Rock. The twins' father had left his family in Nebraska for adventures further west when his sons were only five, never to be heard of again. The lady cousins had hoped to be near each other again and to unite the doctors with Hahn girls. They succeeded with Gary, however Glenn could not bring himself to please his mother and aunt by falling in love with one of his second cousins, perhaps because Gary had managed engage the only good-looking one. At any rate the town benefited greatly by two resident physicians, having previously had medical attention by occasional visiting doctors, midwives, and trips into Kansas City. From this small town the doctors traveled the countryside, to see patients, and most likely, also in search of a wife for Glenn. There was much giggling by women and smirking by men at the sight of the twins on a tandem cycle as they would make visits to patients in the small town, their car reserved for longer trips. Although taken seriously as physicians, and admired by Flat Rock for giving "double duty" care for the sick, the doctors Muller were somewhat the town clowns, light-hearted and funny.

Flat Rock seemed on the verge of losing the unmarried twin until a friendship blossomed between Cora and Glenn. The doctor had visited the Quinn farm when Ella was ill on the night the Heath house burned. He made frequent visits to attend to Ella and when the patient was recovered he would be seen regularly in Cora's store. A distant and proper friendship did grow between shopkeeper and the doctor through the winter, even though gossip about the two queer women was known to Glenn. This did not kill interest in Cora. His self-esteem seemed to need the challenge of winning a woman away from a woman. Glenn and Cora began to be seen on the bicycle built for two whenever the weather permitted and roads were dry enough.

The winter season uncovered mutual admiration between Ella and her niece. The tutorial sessions revealed to each of them the intelligence they shared, along with stories about Ted and Lizzy. Not unadmittedly these two were beginning to revel in the notions of blood relations and much needed mending of tears for which neither was to blame. When Nan revealed to her aunt that she had been able to beat Katie at "Jack Stones" games, and Ella admitted she always managed to beat her sister Bess at the same game, Ella pushed aside the school books, rushing upstairs to return with a much-treasured leather pouch which held the precious stones and rubber ball to start a game played in the middle of the floor! The same stones and ball with which her mother had played did not throw Nan into sadness, but rather seemed to spread infectious laughter throughout the room as Sadie came to them to see why these two were expressing such glee.

Entrance into the Quinn house was no longer an intrusion. Ned would often escort his lover to her sessions with Ella where the three of them would cover the material for testing without antagonism. A walkin fireplace, on scale and in proportions with the large rooms and hallways, often lit by Sadie and kindled by Otis, gave warmth and comfort for the expectation of a new life from Nan's body. It was here with Ella that Ned decided he and his bride would return to the Oklahoma Cane farm for a reunion when summer was over, to give news of a baby on the way! It was time to plan the return. Less than one hundred and fifty miles, just over the Oklahoma border where the Arkansas River flows from Kansas to the "Sooner" land, the land of the "South Winds"

Indians as well as the Creeks, the runaway son would introduce his wife to his family and birthplace. Two more seasons seemed an eternity to wait.

Ralph Hahn delighted in the arrival of two grandsons. Two of his daughters gave birth to baby boys. Nan, offering to help the mothers in order to prepare herself for motherhood, resigned from her work at the asylum, leaving Ned to continue there until June.

Flat Rock seemed to deny any melancholy bleakness of cold months until Charlie Wilkins shot his children, his wife, and himself dead on a late March night during a full moon. To the Canes' surprise Ella burst into unrelenting sobs when she heard of the tragedy. She had not cried, to anyone's knowledge, when Bess had died, or even when her parents had driven off the river bridge three years ago, killing them both. Puzzled by her weeping, which lasted two days and nights, Nan concluded that Cora's announced plan to leave town with Dr. Muller had left her aunt emotionally unarmed. She told Ned it was good riddance to bad rubbish because she could not bear the shopkeeper's flashing her new "in" words. Everything was "so peachy," when the *Ladies' Home Journal* would offer Cora the latest jargon of the big-city girls, suggesting that Cora's dreams for her future would take her to Chicago or New York to see fancy fashions and the fulfillment of a fantasy of marching down Fifth Avenue with thousands of women pushing for the right to vote. Marriage to a doctor could take her nearer to that fulfillment. Besides, Cora's flirtations, although not intentionally aimed at Ned, were turned on whenever a male was in her presence. Nan was glad to see her go.

When Cora moved away, having sold her shop to the Ford garage owner's daughter, Ella invited Ned and Nan to come for supper after their chores were done. An explanation was due, a catharsis, a calming outlet for the hurting woman. After the meal she readily sketched out, as on a private canvas, her tale of heartbreak.

As a teenager, the elder sister, plainer than the exuberant younger Bess, had been found by Charlie Wilkins as she was walking on her family's property. It was a summer day, Wilkins and his two brothers were regular workers on Quinn's farm. Ella had admired Charlie working in the summer sun, browned and shirtless, and like all the Wilkins boys, muscular. Walking to sit on the enormous flat rock on the farm, the rock for which the town was named, Charlie caught up to her and asked, "Is it okay if I walk with you, Ella?"

"Sure, why not?" she said. As the two sat on the hot and smooth rock, two rumps beginning to absorb the heat, and faces steaming under the sun, Charlie reached to hold Ella's face in his hands and place a kiss on her lips. This was a Protestant boy! Ella was terrified and awed ... she kissed him back. This rock became their summer kissing place and though innocent enough, the teens declared their love would last through the necessary temporary secrecy. The rock was a spectacle, only a yard's step up in the highest place and a good one-hundred feet long by forty feet wide. The curving sides of organic form kept the rock from being a hard rectangle. The surface of the rock was smooth and flat overall, creating a playground or dance arena. It was known as a natural oddity around the region. The Quinns, after acquiring the land, had opened the area twice a year for public picnics. This was a place where Bess would bring her daughters and would see her sister and parents, although at arms' length, at picnic time. This was the place where the Kansas River touched the edge of the Quinn's land, bordering it for less than two hundred yards only to turn away abruptly.

Charlie did not return to school. He had gotten another girl in the town pregnant and had to marry. There was no other man for Ella as the years passed, turning Charlie into a no-account drunk. He was, she felt, as heartbroken as she. This man was a pathetic figure, hanging around the Ford garage wearing a Cadillac escutcheon on a string around his neck. Tom Heath realized his neighbor stared at the red Cadillac as it was taken out and as it was returned to the Heath's garage. The secret summer kisses were the romance Ella carried as fantasies for most of her lonely life. Now she had told some-one and her listeners cried with her.

What if Ted and Lizzy had learned of the romance at the rock? What if it had been she who became pregnant? Charlie had been too proper ... she had wished for more. What if Charlie had converted to Catholicism ... to win favor and the comfortable life belonging to the Quinn family? What if he had learned more in school and with her help had spoken better English? What if, what if--Ella reviewed the questions for years until Charlie killed himself and until Ella learned Glenn's story of having treated both Charlie and his wife for syphilis from the time he and his twin arrived in town. No one knew of this so no gossip had spread. After the shoot-ings Glenn had broken the ethics of confidentiality yet had somehow mended Ella's broken spirit and ended her wasted yearnings.

Weeks later, with hesitation, the Lutheran minister called at the Quinn farm to share a scribbled note mailed to the church late on the evening when Charlie decided to take his life along with his family's. Charlie addressed the minister, reading,

"God forgive me for my drunken years and for never doing nothin' for nobody that was good. Mostly forgive me 'cause I had smelt gas around that Heath house before it burned ... it burnt 'cause I threw some matches into that kitchen towards that gas burner ... I murdered them folks ... and the Devil will shore git me now. Don't know why I done it ... just jealous ... maybe jealous of folks who had some loving and a Cadillac ... always wanted one, or maybe I was so drunk I was full of hate. I seen them dirty drawings in that work shed and reckon nobody knows about them ... I could have burned them down too but was too drunk maybe. I had nothing, so gave my wife nothing good, only trouble. Me and my brothers fucked some animals when we wuz young. I wuz the onliest one got sick and passed it on. Maybe the Quinn and the Heath girls should know. You decide."

It was signed more formally than he ever spoke; Charles Evan Wilkins, a native of Kansas. His penmanship was incongruous with his life; correct, beautifully spaced and flowing with an aesthetic flare. The normal-school trained teachers of the time served the public well even in the smallest hamlets.

Spring was late coming so that many suppers with Ella would find Nan and her tutors reading over the secret journals of Tom Heath! It seemed so right to Nan that they were now friendly when Ned eagerly read the journal pages aloud for the two women. As passages were read a discussion would always follow, leaving Ella wishing she had known her brother-in-law who wrote,

"What kept me from a focus? Two drives in scattered units of production. Two passions; one pursued alone to make visions and move color which give form to emotions and energy; the other to serve God, reaching out to find and teach peacefulness. Both offer ecstatic states of mind. The seductions of both require more than one life for perfect blending ... or perhaps a saint's soul with the mind of a genius!"

Ella had never seen the drawings, but when she responded so positively to Tom's words, Nan decided to risk opening the door of the studio to the judgmental Catholic aunt, who had been estranged from the Heaths for so many years ... a separation determined by religious differences. Nan felt deeply that such biases would never split people or families over art, only over religion. Tom had referred to a philosopher once in Nan's company who insisted that fine art values transcend good and evil. Nan had not, and still did not understand the concept. Her perception and decision to show the drawings proved to be correct in furthering the two women in their anticipations of a future to reclaim their kinship. Nan's aunt stood motionless, turning from one point to take in the enormity of the surprise. She kept silent for most of an hour, occasionally searching for Nan's eyes which were focused on items in a box in the back of the journals' closet. There she found a woman's driving duster with price tag of $2.95, and a pair of lady's goggles, priced at $.50, both from Saks in New York. Envisioning a red-headed woman in a red car, she closed the box and replaced it, thinking these had been put away for Christmas. On the bottom shelf were cans labeled "linseed oil," "turpentine," and "stand oil," along with large granules of rabbit skin glue and jars of white lead powder needed for sizing pieces of linen which were rolled around thinly milled strips of lumber. These materials had waited for Tom's courage to move beyond graphics to painting.

Ella whispered a response to the drawing. "How beautiful ... how beautiful, how beautiful!" They left quietly together.

In a white heat of June, which seemed to take spirit out of even the younger children in the Midwestern new season for bare feet, mothers checked at sunset for ringworm and ticks. One wondered not that the lingering ices had delayed spring in the small town until late April or that so suddenly the heat saw children claiming their earth contact by closeting their shoes to run in warm sands and dust. As the June procession began across the newly cut greens, the wonderment was that Nan marched in the graduation procession and would be acknowledged as an honor student. She was in the third month of her pregnancy, feeling freer and happier than she could ever remember. The atomizer was no longer under her pillow for asthmatic seizures. Her courage to live, work, and love was stronger than she could have imagined. Ella attended the ceremony and was genuinely proud of her niece.

On graduation day in his childlike jocose style, Ned suggested that school notebooks not be stacked in attics or carted away to dark corners of dusty places. His proposal had a definite edge. Nan jumped at it. Hand-in-hand, they ran to a bluff overlooking the river where they ripped the pages of her senior year notes into hundreds of pieces, scaling them into the rushing waters below. The scraps had a more poetic ending than anything therein inscribed.

"Oh, Ned, let's never stop running ... our cycles, horses, cars, don't compare with the splendor of our feet taking our bodies and souls through space. Life must be shorter sitting on butts and longer on our toes!

"Well, could we just walk fast until the baby comes, and then pick up the pace?" Once again they were off for a race into the landscape of their lives. Their run would be a long one.

9

Finding Flat Rock

Before leaving the eastern seaboard in 1873, on a journey designed to venture towards the pacific Ocean, a seminarian classmate of Ted's married the runaway religionists. The groom was thirty-three. The bride was twenty-five when they left all the family they knew, and their homes, in Baltimore and Savannah. In late summer of 1873 the newlyweds were on a train to Chicago en route to Kansas City. Their outlook was optimistic and bright with every reason to believe their travel would be easy since the Overland California Mail Bill had, since 1867, made deliveries possible, the Pony Express had been running mail to San Francisco before that, and railroads were fast covering the United States.

In Kansas City Ted scurried to the bank to confirm that monies had been transferred to set up an account for him with limits only relative to the total capital for amounts he might withdraw, and with a schedule for regular withdrawals; then on to register into a decent hotel and spruce up for Monday evening mass at the Catholic church. To their surprise, colored and white people were at mass together and on the front steps of the church after mass a large black man approached them asking whether they would need a hired man. He was looking for work. He and his wife had been in the city almost a year, up from Mississippi, and had not been able to secure any lasting jobs. They were Otis and Sadie Banks, who had tried sharecropping but found too much hatred left over from pre-confederacy treatment of Negroes. They had relatives on plantations in the South still laboring with shackles. Lizzy said many times in years to come that God had sent these two to them at the church doors. Knowing that he would need a strong co-worker and good scout, whatever they might encounter on their westward move, Ted agreed to find a way to employ Otis. When pondering the privilege of experiencing, first hand, the enormity of America by a few days' venture into Kansas, Ted accepted a plan for the new servants to collect the Quinns from the hotel the next morning in the horse-drawn wagon that Otis had managed to hold onto because Lizzy cleaned rooms in a flophouse in the colored section. The next order of business was to purchase a suitable horse and carriage, for heading west to a place where Otis had found work in fields recently. Two couples, one in a wagon to lead the other in a fashionable carriage.

Only a few miles out of town, the road leaving the city connected with the Old Trail which could lead one all the way to Oregon, or, within an hour, to an offshoot road which led into Flat Rock. The ride delighted Lizzy as white feather-like puffs blew through winds around the carriage, leaving the white leaves of the cottonwood trees which she would learn to love as she loved the magnolia trees of the southland. She squeezed Ted's arm and almost swooned when white-tail deer leaped across fields and occasional sunflowers seemed to be reaching heights to overtake the tall corn. This was still frontier territory to two Easterners, although as early as the 1860s land grants and homestead acts offered acres of land to men over twenty-one who would squat, grow timber, clear the land for farming, and earn the right to buy, after several years, land at sometimes as little as one to two dollars an acre. The national government's interest in promoting settlements westward continued until the turn of the century.

Gas lines were in place, in the center of Flat Rock, but

River Bend Hotel

not to farmers who still relied on kerosene lanterns. Water systems had not replaced outhouses, even though the town was relatively close to Kansas City. It would be more than a decade before AT&T would provide Lizzy with a telephone, two decades before she would see the one-room elementary and high school building expanded to two rooms with a cafeteria, thirty years before crappers would be installed in a few of the homes in the community, and forty years before Coca-Cola trucks would be making deliveries even in the smallest villages.

It never occurred to Ted, as they reached the River Bend Hotel, that he and his wife would fall in love with Kansas, particularly the acreage they would buy, work hard, and love, instead of traveling on to the Pacific to settle in a city only to resume lives similar to ones they had known in comfort and with money. Lizzy knew little of cooking or surviving outside of a convent. Sadie was a great cook, who knew how to survive, being born to parents born into slavery. Ted knew nothing of farming. Otis was a master at it.

Upon arrival at the hotel it was clear to the Quinns that the colored couple was known in these premises. When Otis had worked in the cornfields Sadie had worked in the kitchen of the hotel and the owner of the River Bend had let them stay in a room behind the kitchen while there was work for Otis.

When having dinner in the hotel that first night in Flat Rock, a Widow Morris introduced herself to the Quinns and related her story of having taken advantage of the government's gift of acreage in the Midwest to widows of the Civil War soldiers. She had taken the land, and, several years later, traveled from New Jersey with her two young sons to stay. Now she wished to sell sixty-four of the 165 acres deeded to her and urged the Quinns to at least look at the plot which bordered The Old Trail and was touched by the river. The vivacious delivery of her story and her sprightly movements were so engaging the Quinns joined the widow's table to dine with the two young Morris boys and their mother. The boys were quiet as they ate with rather fine manners while their mother was loquacious and witty, ostensibly at ease socially.

Next morning Otis walked the widow's land with Ted and Lizzy while Sadie helped in the hotel to earn the Banks' board. The hopeful seller greeted the prospective buyers in black mourning clothes with a dour mood as complement. Otis had warned Ted of the widow's swings in mood and manner because people said she had worn black clothes for eight years whenever she wished to appear helpless and victimized, yet on other occasions of business she was brightly colored in both attire and spirit as she wheeled aggressively any deal to her benefit. Flat Rock's citizens were merely cordial to her because she talked out loud to herself and was accepted as crazed. Luckily she seemed to need no friends.

Ted bought the land in an agreement which felt to him to be a divinely planned move. Lizzy was drunk with the beauty of Kansas fields and the stand of gigantic black walnut trees, left uncut because they were too tough to fell. Otis informed her that when the dark green shells of the nuts were ready to fall away gloves must be worn to crack and pick the meat. Otherwise her hands would be stained dark brown. In his never-overbearing suggestions, he let her know that long sleeves would be needed when she spied some gooseberries for their stem came with sharp barblike spines. Over the coming years Sadie and Lizzy would go gathering to make reputedly the best gooseberry pies in Kansas.

Although the Morris property had been farmed, Ted bought a hundred more acres adjoining it which had to be partly cleared. Some local farmers in need of work helped with the clearing for building the Quinns' home and the Banks' cabin. As more hands were needed in the beginning Otis brought colored crews from Kansas City to live in dugouts with good ground cover and blankets at night. Food was bountiful where Sadie made her home and she doled it out generously. The August heat was unrelentingly scorching, causing sunflowers, which covered fields and gardens, to drop their heavy heads more than usual and break from their stems. Yellow petals were curled by burned edges. The temperature was cruel by day but a blessing to workers by night in the hillside dugouts which could have been bone-chilling around midnight.

Old wells had to be reclaimed near the dugouts as well as near the home site. In 1868 wells had been filled in viciously by Wilkins men, uncles of Charlie Wilkins, when word got out that Widow Morris was on her way to claim her grant. The Wilkins had squatted on the land to hunt and do small farming, so when officials threw them off "their" land they found ways, though not life-threatening, to make life hard for the rightful owner. She arrived, having survived the death of her husband in the war, with two young sons and a brother. She would stand up to harassing but the brother, who was once dragged two hundred yards across a field tied to a Wilkins mule and cut free in a mud hole, stayed a year and returned to the East.

Ted Quinn's insight and wisdom in diplomacy earned him fast acceptance in the town. First of all, farmers were glad to work on his land. Secondly, when colored workers came with Otis to help there was no resentment in the community because Ted paid the Kansas City crew a day or two extra to stay and assist farmers who might need extra hands, claiming the farmers would do him a favor to use them since he had promised more days' work to entice the colored men to come to Flat Rock. The fact is they would have come any time to have work and money and food. The former priest was never unmindful of mistrust of, and prejudice against,

Catholics west of the eastern seaboard of America, so gave attention to being a good neighbor.

The first year his crops were harvested, whether corn or hay, Ted delivered donations to each church in the community for their "church banks," his way of tithing for any emergency of drought or other disasters killing crops. He established a tradition of appearing through a window in the primary school grades to play Santa Claus, bringing large red bags filled with toys, candied apples, and popcorn. Occasionally an orange, at the time truly a luxury, could be produced for a teacher.

Ted continued his good-neighbor deeds not in dishonesty, but in genuine desire to act for the good of his chosen town. Although not interested in owning large herds of cattle, he sent workers to assist farmers when they needed barbed wire, first known as 'bobwarr" and first used by farmers to protect crops by keeping animals out of their fields and off their land. By 1880 fifteen million horses were reported to be owned by Americans, some for hauling both short land loads as well as long-distance freight. By 1886 Texas drives had increased beef cattle heads to four million in Kansas, Colorado, Nebraska, Wyoming, and Montana. When ranches became large spreads, barbed wire was used to keep cattle in, but not as absolute protection. "Night riders" would cut the wire to steal steers. Several states gave hanging penalties to horse thieves. Flat Rock's interest in the wire was always to keep the animals out.

Farmers were at the mercy of nature's whims. They would prepare as best they knew how and then hope that grasshoppers would not appear to ravage crops, that the winter snows and winds would be mild enough to allow the hay, so vital for feeding animals, to thrive. And then, of course, there was the real culprit and threat to farming, the droughts. In 1891, out of Goodland, Kansas, an Irishman named Melbourne was reported to have called up rain clouds. The Interstate Artificial Rain Corporation negotiated with him to purchase his secret for making rain. Drought-stricken states in mid-America had seen his magic succeed but also fail. Results seemed a toss of the dice and divining rods, sticks with a "wish-bone" shape, used by "water witches," had been more consistent in dowsing sub-waters than rainmakers in calling up rain clouds. Still, only one success could bring fortunes to anyone with talent at guessing.

In 1893 Ted Quinn brought Melbourne to Flat Rock after persistent droughts. The Irishman brought rain for three days so that forever after Ted and his family were considered homefolks.

The Hahns had the history and the land.

The Quinns had a new home, and coming from the East as Catholics with money but a lack of "airs" and arrogance, their love of Kansas land and hard work made it easy for Flat Rock to accept them.

During their settling, after Ted and Lizzy had studied manuals for building plans, they decided that Otis would be their source of information, schooled by experience in farming, using and repairing farm equipment, and in construction. The Quinns' plan was a continuous string of subsidiary buildings connected to the main house by a covered breezeway. A few steps through this connection would bring one to the spring house, then the woodshed, the milk house, the tool house, and the chicken coops. Although silos were on farms by 1870, Ted chose to have a grain barn attached to his separate crib barn for animals, carriages, and equipment. The hog, sheep and goat pens were furthest from the house to distance the smells. Otis was the master teacher and Ted was a fast learner. In the house Sadie was the teacher and Lizzy the student. There were no "bosses," but rather a quartet of genuine friends. Down in Mississippi, Sadie had been raped by a black

67

Quinn's Place

plantation worker who happened to be a lead worker. Otis interrupted the attacker in the act, and killed his wife's abuser with his pants down. Otis's huge hands found this attacker's neck easy enough to break. Since then the plantation owner was bent on finding Otis to watch him swing from a tree for murdering his best laborer, Otis was on the run for the rest of his life.

Instead of a gambrel roof barn Otis designed a crib barn with a tall steep-roofed middle section and two attached wings of lower heights and more gradually sloping roofs. White oak beams were hand-hewn. Hemlock and pine were used for siding and red stain for the barn, chosen to retain more heat in colder months. Instead of bark slabs slate shingles were put overhead on the main house and barn. The slate from Arkansas, called red, with a pink appearance and said to have been in the ground for over a hundred million years, brought town folks to see the unusual roof but they understood that this choice was not for "show" but for greater fireproofing. The other structures had tin roofs, giving a variation of sounds at rainfalls making country life more enrapturing to the Quinns who were accustomed to wooden shingles. Beauty of craft, down to the wooden "tree nails" used to join beams, was recognized by barn builders who came from fifty miles around to see what the black man knew.

Although Kansas newspapers had cast an eye of mistrust of Catholics by reporting that a social fraternity established as the Knights of Columbus was unpatriotic, the Quinns were trusted by their neighbors. They stayed, had children, and never regretted having stopped just west of Kansas City. Otis and Sadie had made this settlement possible. The Bankses likewise felt blessed that they had found a safe place to call home. Hard-working farmers followed traditions of giving sons essentials to start their out "on their own" when they got married. The usual gifts were a few acres of land if possible, or money enough to lease a plot for a year, along with a horse, mule, wagon, harnesses, bridles, and halters. Ted Quinn gave the Banks these gifts plus sixty-four of his acres. The gesture was formalized by a deed recorded in Kansas City but kept quiet in order to hold back resentment in whites.

Sadie's shock in life, leaving her childless, came in the second summer of the Quinn's farming. Having come to call Otis and workers to supper as a storm approached she decided to stand on the big flat rock near the river's edge to call them. Before she could climb the rock lighting struck her to the ground. Otis saw her fall and, racing to lift her seemingly boneless body, sagging and limp, he placed her on the rock as Ted, also racing to Sadie, yelled to a worker to take the wagon and get Lizzy.

"Tell Mrs. Quinn to bring my special black case!!!"

Ted took Sadie in his arms and began to speak in foreign words of low tones of prayer in memorized and regular metered content to an apparently lifeless woman. Within minutes Lizzy jumped from the returning wagon, placed a stole around Ted's shoulders and handed him a silver vial and bible. As she was blessed, then sprinkled with holy water, Sadie slowly opened her eyes. Suddenly her eyes flew wide open and she gasped, "Father?"

As her limp body began to warm a bit, again she asked, "Father?"

"No more, my friend, no more. Never speak of this again."

Otis and Sadie did not speak again of what they knew in a flash that day of the near-fatal flash. They believed her body was left childless from the strike but as Catholics believed she lived by a blessing.

She mothered the Quinn girls. Their teeth were kept whiter than any other children's teeth by her gifts of peeled and sliced deep purple sugar cane when Otis could find it in the colored markets in Kansas City. The girls would chew and suck the sweetness from the cane, cleaning their teeth in the process. Sadie helped them survive many a chigger bite with her water solution and witch hazel, rubbed her "tiger's milk," a potion she acquired from relatives from Trinidad, on chests to cure coughs and colds, and would use her mixture of camphor, wintergreen and mineral oils for aches and pains. Best of all for the girls, as they started school, were Sadie's ghost stories. Otis was even spooked by them and sometimes unable to sleep after an evening of Sadie's tales. No one on the Quinn place suffered from a toothache long when Sadie poured oil of cloves on the spot, and like it or not, she doled out winter preventatives of cod liver oil and blackstrap molasses to all residents of the farm.

Happiness reigned over the farm for two decades. Two daughters were born in the farmhouse. Ella and Bess swam at the river's edge, picked berries, and loved milking the cows, feeding the hogs and chickens and gathering eggs to put in crates. This was not forced upon them, and usually not carried out as required duties twice daily, but enjoyed as fun. Pinafores worn in Baltimore and Savannah were part of the Quinn girls' daily school outfit, not so much as a fashion but as a practical cover which kept dresses cleaner. The white starched aprons caught the fancy of the other country girls who all wanted them. Sadie made them for any girls who really liked them. Ironically, girls from the deep South disliked the pinafores for being to prissy and restricting on playgrounds. Children seemed to emulate Ella and Bess, always eager to visit their farm in all seasons, especially for summer picnics.

At Christmas Otis would make toboggans, help children up onto the barn roof, and see them slide down into high haystacks. Once, Ella climbed higher on the roof than others to gain greater speed, which sent her off the roof and over the haystack. Her leg was injured, leaving her with an uneven walk. The toboggans were wooden frameworks covered with smooth tin, a holding rope, but no brakes. If legs were not used well for braking, nearby hills often sent sledders into thin ice-covered creek beds, and into freezing shallow waters. All were memories of glee in special seasons. There was a long stretch of pleasure and joy. Only undercurrents of hostility could ever account for Ella and Bess failing to demand reconciliation when Tom and Ted had their lasting split. Was it the sisters' competitiveness to be included in that magical, closed, love aura which glued Ted and Lizzy, and of its own power actually excluded to a degree even their own children? Each was all the other deeply needed, and therefore there was no "inclusion" for others in their union of romance. They had their heaven here on earth. It was obvious to everyone who ever saw them together.

10

Bar Room Talk

Most of the men in town could be found at least a couple of evenings a week at the bar room of the River Bend Hotel. It was a place where women and children did not go and where Mr. Quinn, although liked by all, had not been welcome nor had Reverend Heath, perhaps because they would have cramped the raunchy and sometimes profane language of the group. Although a time for arguments of some merit, it was a gathering where idle banter would dominate and such persiflage would not have amused Mr. Quinn, who, loving good wit, may have shown some arrogance here. How unfortunate two men, one the father of Bess, the other her husband, had not talked to each other to exchange good stories while comparing their chosen religions.

The nasty smell in the bar room was not from cigars or even booze, but from the many misses the drinkers had when trying for the spittoon. The stains on the floor told the story not of gun fights or fists fights bringing blood, but rather chewing tobacco missing the receptacles. Those found there were farmers, Widow Morris's two sons, Bob and Bert, the twin doctors, Ralph Hahn, store owners, the pharmacist, and any travelers going through.

Mr. Hahn, having been surrounded his whole life by sisters, surrounded by females, relished these evenings. Once or twice he took Ned, who loved the company of the older men but usually had other priorities. At least he knew he was welcome and enjoyed hearing Ralph as the most outspoken in his responses to local and national politics. There was plenty to kick around in the winter of 1920.

Billy Sunday, an Evangelist preacher, had become famous by hitting the "sawdust circuits" under the big tents converting thousands to Christianity, and had taken sides with supporters of prohibition. Ralph and plenty to say about this guy.

"I'll tell you one thing. This S.O.B. was probably a drunk before he was a preacher. I know he has worked as an assistant in the undertaker business and I can tell you he probably looked at those poor dead folks, when he was preparing them for burial, and said to himself that they had surely done more harm in life than if they had not ever had a drink and that they were doomed earlier because they had been drinkers. But when I prepare dead folks as I did in that flu epidemic, when people had to pay fifty dollars for a gallon of whiskey to get so-called legal alcohol, when hell, we got plenty of stills around here and don't need to go to our friend at the drugstore for the prescription, but I saw those deceased as having been in need of some good stiff drinks to sustain them and maybe even get them over the damn illness. The god-awful government better stop sticking its nose in our business or we could see a revolution."

"Damned right!" piped in the druggist.

"If Wilson's crazy proclamation three years ago to have the government take over operations of the railroads hadn't been overturned last year we would have had a real uprising. Washington ain't so far we can't get there and fire up some riots."

The pharmacist not only provided apothecary needs, tobacco, and spices, but also served as the town's man-midwife before the twin doctors arrived to practice. He also performed some minor surgery and pulled teeth. Everyone in Flat Rock wanted to stay on his good side so that he would come quickly when a baby was on its way, and act as kindly as possible when tooth extractions were necessary.

"Hell, us out here in corn and wheat fields saw the writin' on the wall before the war, that them rail tracks was beginning to strangle farmers with goddam lines all over our land," agreed the Ford garage owner.

Ralph nodded positive here.

"Well, we'll keep our stills and do our drinking, come what may. If we have a hankering to walk nude outside we may do that too!" The group laughed hard, knowing Ralph was referring to Widow Morris' having been reported strolling her property unclothed in bright sunlight because she had read this would prevent her catching the flu two years before.

One of the widow's sons turned red with clenched fists to refute the story.

"You assholes believe everything you hear but if you make more fun of my ma there'll be some broken noses here tonight."

The men apologized for the laughter as the other Morris brother said, "We only know she talked about it herself and walked in such hidden parts of the farm ain't nobody ever gonna know whether she was just spicing up life round here. She sure as hell didn't get the flu and we're never seen her sick a day of our lives. She's going on sixty-eight!"

Both the brothers had volunteered to serve in the U.S. Army and had been sent to France. Being much too old to be drafted when the Selective Service Act was passed, the brothers took themselves into Kansas City to watch a parade for recruitments, and, getting caught up in the passion of patriotism, they volunteered to serve and be committed to universal liability to serve their country. This idea was engraved in the minds of most Americans by James Montgomery Flagg's famous poster bearing the image of Uncle Sam, pointing to viewers and declaring a need for all to defend and fight. The brothers lied to the recruitment officer, declaring their ages to be ten years younger than they were which was still too old for the draft. Actually, looking much younger than their ages and being so eager to enlist, and having come upon an officer who was paid a bonus for every recruit he signed up, whether draftee or volunteer, the brothers became soldiers that day in the city. Bob and Bert had decided that getting out of Flat Rock was exactly what they needed and the Army might just bring them some bragging rights back home. When the folks in the small town heard that these men, forty six and forty eight years of age, had gone to war they were not surprised that the ruffians were going to fight, but wondered how in the world the Army kept them. It was because Bob and Bert worked harder than any other men. They dug ditches, carried supplies and were both master marksmen, having hunted all their lives. Bert had taken a bullet that splintered the acromial end of his clavicle on his right side. Bob had been wounded in his thigh and patella, but healed before returning home. Bert sometimes wore the shirt he had on when he took the bullet, still stained with blood and ripped. He felt lucky to have survived but wanted to claim some heroism. Small towns accept their eccentrics and indeed encourage them for added local color and gossip.

Their mother had driven into the hotel at least three times a week while they were away, to find someone to play the Ouija board so she could ask whether her boys would return safely. One night she would ask about Bob and the next night about Bert. Both of her sons returned with only slight wounds even though they had seen death around them in the foxholes. Their return was a testament to the toughness they gained by growing up on their farm and enduring the hazing of the Wilkins men who had hoped they could drive the Morris family back East, leaving them free to use the land as they had before. Because Bert had once left a farmer who teased him with a bloody nose, the barroom gatherers tiptoed gingerly around their favorite comments from the past about how the Widow's sons worked only for fluff money while living with and "on" their ma's government pension. No wives, babies, responsibilities were theirs except working the family farm.

A farmer now dared a dig, "You better hope she lives another sixty-eight years! Her pension dries up when she does. Maybe some rich sodbuster will have daughters for you. Hahn had a bunch who wouldn't have you even tho you both so good-looking!"

More grins and belly laughs came as that farmer bought Bert and Bob drinks, proving that he was more than a little nervous about the possibility of taking some blows to his head. The brothers were the two among the denizens at the hotel who regularly got pie-eyed before disbanding. The glow of gaslights and occasional kerosene lanterns in the bar always rekindled the groups' concern about whether they would get electrical service on farms before they died. Their concerns were realistic. As late as 1935 nine out of ten farms would still not have electricity even though these farmers had seen the overland railroad cars across flat acres change from gas lights to electric lights in 1905, when generated steam from engines drove power throughout the trains.

They argued whether Ford, having reduced the production time of a car from thirteen hours to six, would be able to reduce the assembly production time even more, and fantasized about robots taking over both world auto making and farm labor. Being especially thick-tongued in late hours, their projections could have been scripts for successful science fiction books at mid-twentieth century. Their talk, although not intellectual, was born of common and profound issues on the minds of all urban and rural Americans.

"Women are stronger beasts! Stronger than us ... don't

kid yo'selves that you can outlive 'em," the druggist exclaimed angrily.

"First thing you know they'll be running the country, not just inside our houses, now that they got the vote … God love Tennessee, 'cause that state was the last to ratify gals' right to vote. We'll have to turn that around too. They have the right to own property and that's the last straw. They ought to be kept like children, asking permission for everything." Applause could be heard from the hotel as each man was tilting his third or fourth beverage. By now the men were loose enough to release sulfurous gases freely when needed. The spittoons no longer dominated the atmosphere.

"Well, you won't even find Widow Morris asking anybody for permission for anything … when the enemies come over our hills I sho as hell want her on my side … whether she's in her high mood or one when she lets out words a sailor can't match! She's a fine character to be dealt with and could have had a man through all the years when she chose to stay unwed … 'course her pension from the government would be a magnet," added Ralph, bringing more laughter shared even by the widow's sons. Everyone in the town was aware the womenfolk avoided the widow, whose acrimonious mood could, with language, make faces look and feel as though bees had stung one's cheeks.

Dr. Gary Muller strolled into the bar, catching the last comment.

"Well, Widow Morris takes care of herself! I know two years ago when the flu was killing folks, we couldn't get anyone to wear the gauze masks except her. The bar sold plenty of booze cause people believed it would save them and they would not be one of the every four persons in the country infected with what they called Spanish flu. My brother and I remember out here in the Kansas camp soldiers were turning blue and dying within days but that was before anyone connected the hell with Spain!"

He ordered whiskey and continued, "Speaking of foreign places ... I hear the government is talking about curbing the number of immigrants from Europe and elsewhere by setting quotas. I know that ten years ago, forty percent of New York's population was foreign-born."

Ethan, who had owned the Ford garage in town, began teasing one of the farmers in the bar,

"Listen, sodbuster, ain't you ever gonna buy a car? You gonna be the last man in the county to travel with yo' mule? Ford says the vibrations in the quiver are good for the liver ... you could live to be a hundred."

"Naw ... my daddy called them things devil wagons and I believe him. Besides, it's a lie that a fuckin' car is easier to keep up than an animal. My mule ain't ever been sick!"

Ethan, who was known to be annoyed by population growth since a newcomer was planning on opening a second filling station in Flat Rock, chimed in, "Well, I hope to hell Harding is elected by just sitting on his front porch through the campaign like he says he will! The Republicans have the right man this time, 'cause he says to hell with the League of Nations ... just take care of our own country."

Dr. Gary responded, "Yeah, they sent his girl friend to some place in South America before the news spread through out the country that he was running around, you know what I mean, so all the news that this man wants serenity by putting America first is probably his need for more peace in his own household ... his old lady will have him sitting on the front porch for a long time."

"He may have to go to the White House in ball and chains," said Hahn, wrapping up an ordinary evening of the men with a roar of laughter.

11

A Homecoming

Ned's earliest impression of his father were of great pressures to be on guard, to duck and race away from swinging arms and hands, while longing to be embraced lovingly. The paternal arms often hit their mark, leaving bruises on all of the Cane boys. It was early fall, as the red Cadillac crossed the creaking wooden bridge on the Cane property, the bridge which had echoed the clapping of horse hooves bringing James home after many a late night's cavorting ... the bridge that had transmitted a sedative sound for a mother's sleep because James was safe. James was home.

Ned shuddered, knowing James would never be home again. He glanced at the gold wristwatch.

Nan sat up, bracing herself on the bumpy ride over a rocky road to the house. Discomfort from legs in a seated position, pushing up against the swelling belly, would increase now until the birth. Her slender body silhouetted an image of expectancy as she carried a high delicate bulge in her sixth month. Her dark hair was shinier than ever in the September sun around a complexion glistening as though pastel lanolin had been sprayed all over her.

From a woods fifty yards from the house Ned recognized a figure emerging from tall red cedars, staggering toward their car and shouting, "Mama! Mama! The boy's home, Mama!" A shrunken giant, groping to hold his balance to stand, fell forward to hit the dirt. Charlotte Cane bounded from the

80

front porch of the Cane farmhouse waving to Ned while rushing to the fallen man, whose hardening brain was slipping into darkness, a mental tunnel where cognitive lights were being squeezed from dimness to blackness.

The son leaped from his car to be surprised by the ease of lifting a diminished David Cane, who, when on his feet, sobbed and reached to kiss Nan. The foursome moved towards the house in a grey mood lifted by colored fall leaves not yet crunchy under feet. Pity instantly overcame the hatred so long harbored by Ned, who had sent word by Jake Moon that he was to tell his mother that September would bring him and his wife home. Homecoming would become a glorious reunion in which flushed past pains and emerging future hopes would help love catch up to time lost.

Charlotte had not even tried to send word of her husband's deterioration over the two years since Ned left. The first year David's slurring speech and gradual loss of balance came rather slowly, at a creeping snail's pace, so close to their everyday living, only provoking alarm in Charlotte when he would fall in the fields or drop his eating utensils regularly. Ned's sadness seemed not so much for his father, but for the heavy burden his mother had carried alone. Perry, after moving to live on a lake some five miles away, had seldom come home to the farm, finding it too difficult to see the abusive giant fade into a frightening although peaceful isolation. Perry had stayed on the farm the longest.

The home place was a sadder picture than Jake had painted. Meadows were overgrown with old hay still standing or beaten down by weather. Crops had been neglected for over a year because the Canes could not pay local Indians to work the land. Two milk cows and two steers were the only animals left in the gambrel-roofed barn. Even the sheep and goats had been sold so that little grazing had cleared meadows. A hay wain threshing machine, bridles, harnesses, pitch forks and wagons were still usable and enough in number for hired hands to work the land. Ned would spend much of his time during the two-week visit finding and recruiting, with Jake, Kaw Indians in need of food along with promises of money. The big job of persuasion was to press Perry to return home to oversee and help with the restoration of the property. The fisherman did not say yes.

Mrs. Cane's tender gestures in the care of her husband came from a slab of time being rolled back, giving her reminders of the handsome man who had seized her heart, the man folks said could walk through a brick outhouse, who could single-handedly hogtie five good men. She now had a sixth "son" to care for in the way she had raised her five sons, and welcomed the new guardianship because she gained her darling again. He required assistance even to the outhouse, with his loss of independence bringing a loss of dignity. Charlotte clung to the man and memories of her youth, memories of two lovers finding their splendor in high grasses and between corn rows on the hundred-acre, prosperous farm belonging to her parents, parents who rejected David and his parents because they were very poor. Her story was not unique. She and David eloped to have each other with a life of passion and hard labor, laboring for others. They were happy.

As an only child, Charlotte inherited the farm and the house full of expensive rugs and furnishings, a house, although large enough for a family of seven, which failed to match the quality of the furnishings. Droughts came in successive years which necessitated the sale of much of Charlotte's furniture, gradually. Not so gradually David became a drunkard. Hard times failed to attack Charlotte's stamina and good spirits. Her five sons were her salvation in joy. By the time the third son was born any money the father came by was spent on liquor. Ned and Nan realized that Charlotte chose to dwell on love regained, with demonstrated affection in both glances and kisses. Ned could not recall ever having seen this look of love between them, or the happiness his parents shared at a time when one of them was sinking into mental mud.

In the evenings conversations were precious especially to mother and son. "How were you able to keep the house when the farm wasn't even producing, Ma?" Ned's guilt was eating at him for staying away so long, for just waiting for a chance to return and free his mother of abuse from a powerful figure. Clearly his mother was not experiencing care for David as onerous tasks.

"You noticed I did not sell the piano? Well, I also have well-hidden gems ... some jewelry left to me by my mother. I really think the brief but excellent studies I had at a private girls' school before I fell for your dad kept me sane through dreaming, reading, and enjoying my music, but beyond that I got my grandmother's wisdom to survive. By the way, Nan, this is the grandmother whose recipe for cornbread you admired. I'll copy this for you before you leave ... this bread will stick to your bones when eaten at breakfast."

Because the young pregnant daughter-in-law knew that Mother Cane, as she called her, could comprehend her father's writings, she brought out one of the journals of her dead father and asked Ned to read to the family each night during their visit.

"Everything is in the composition. The nothingness of white space demands reverence as should a perfect silence. Will it result in mistake or brilliance when that space is broken? By turning the paper or canvas to a horizontal or vertical emphasis some perplexing problems begin. If the diagonal seems indecisive or neutral, the vertical active and energized, the sweeping horizontal vistas seem to me, in the most aesthetic forms, highly energized also. Vistas in consuming gentleness take and hold ... this is not without aggressiveness. To lie down is not to die but to dream, to reproduce and know ecstasy. Energized horizontals are not barren plateaus but complex possibilities that test the courage of any artist. The challenge is to resolve inevitable ambiguities as palatable contradictions."

This was not the writing of an unschooled country preacher. Early in his life Tom's parents had impressed on him a curiosity of ideas, language, and sophisticated style for approaching all intellectual questions.

Jake Moon and Ned went to work at clearing some of the meadows and paths through the woods. More workers were needed to merely get crop acres cleared before another winter. Jake and his family had not known a day free of fear for their freedom or free of fear for their lives. If Indians wished to move in any direction to seek safety they faced the same threats of all persons considered "foreigners" or simply not "belonging" to "one's kind," threats growing from hatred, especially if they were not of the same race or religion. Midwestern Indians had been given land by the government in 1914 only to see it taken back, and eventually put under federal control. Political and church leaders received similar threats when opposing the KKK. Lynchings were harbingers of eventual need for imposing state martial law as well as activation of National Guards. This was the country into which Jake had been born, a land which had promised freedom and the pursuit of happiness, but had not made good on the promise spoiled by intolerance.

At the age of six Jake had witnessed the lynching of a Kaw Indian who had merely driven a wagon over the Oklahoma border searching for relatives. A lawless crowd had blamed the Kaw for the burning of a barn full of cows, a fire which also had taken the life of a farm hand trying to save the animals. Actually, when entering the village the Kaw had a pet bulldog with him that had run up too close to a mule's rear, barking. The mule had kicked up, clipping the pug's head and causing the dog to react by jumping high, closing his teeth and locking his jaw on the mule's throat. Men on the street pulled on the pug only to see more and more blood lost by the larger animal which put forth agonizing hee-haws followed by groaning whimpers, its life slowly ebbing. Gaping onlookers watched legs of the suffering ass begin to buckle as the bulldog's eyes widened, enlarging the whites of his eyeballs to a startling size in expression of terror. A clerk from the trading post and general store hurried toward the incident to shoot the dog for a release of the canine's clamped teeth. Both animals died. For weeks the oiled dirt street held a reminder in the crimson color where both creatures had floated in blood. Having lot his mule, a farmer fabricated the story that he had seen the Indian sneaking around the barn which had burned the day before. That farmer struck the match which fired up an angry, event-hungry crowd.

Jake had described the public horror to Ned with details of the victims' eyes popping out of his skull since no burlap "croaker" sack had been placed over his head for some last moment of dignity. It was a tale Ned would ask Jake to repeat many times when the two boys, promising each other to always be a helping hand to people in need, paddled in their canoes to rescue folks from flooded homes. This opportunity came often as the Arkansas River and Turkey Creek would flood leaving families stranded in rising waters. How young to be heroes! The natural "high" which came to the boys saving lives carved in them a permanent tendency to kindness. This unspoken yet understood pledge was to never choose the cruelty of the Klan.

Perry came home three days before Ned and Nan were to leave. He arrived with an Indian squaw whom he had married by Indian law, the reason he had stayed away from his parents who would have been in possible danger. Intolerance in this case demanded that Cherry, the squaw, would be presented to folks, coming to and fro at the Canes, as a servant living in the home to help Mrs. Cane. It would be several years before Perry and his family could, or would, although loving the girl, be able to claim her for their own. Again prejudice and intolerance could dictate how citizens could live in love, but could never gain power to dictate whom to love. Ned quietly laughed with Nan about the rhyming names and for years she would occasionally call him Dan.

On their ride back to Flat Rock Nan enjoyed looking through her father's journal and knew that Mother Cane would read them with Ella and herself some day. Glancing at the cornbread recipe she read the name Martha Davis, and in fading ink but fancy penmanship, "from the oven of Martha Davis Seltzer, 1820 Savannah, Georgia." Nan remembered that Lizzy Quinn had come from Savannah. How wonderful, she thought, to find my Grandmother's past ... and maybe my grandfather's relatives. She knew Ted had folks in Baltimore she wished to know about. Less than a year ago she had whispered to Ned, on the night of the fire, "I have no folks!"

12

Denouement

Jazz was beginning to be labeled immoral and decadent after World War I, and connected to Negro salons. But in Kansas City "hot houses" played it. Protégées of Scott Joplin were developing novel indigenous musical forms which were enjoyed clandestinely by both whites and blacks. Jim Crow laws were in force throughout the country, creating atmospheres wherein blacks needed hidden places for enjoying their beats and dance rhythms with whites. Otis and Sadie, having no children, and having Negro company only at times when work crews were needed, would wind up the victrola back in their cabin, place the needle on the record, and hear sounds that were theirs. There was enough land and space for their safety. Nan and Ned ventured to the Banks's home upon returning from Oklahoma to accept Sadie's invitation to come for chokeberry wine, fish, hushpuppies, and jazz. They convinced Ella to come along, and to their surprise she got tipsy and moved to the music as even Otis had not seen. Sadie knew that having minded both Bess and Ella as babies through their growing up, and having sung gospel with tambourines, these girls would always connect to the colored music. Ella's motor memory, when she became high on wine, led her to dance the way she did as a toddler, to Sadie's drumming with a metal spoon on a number-two wash tub.

The fall air had a chill but a fire outside the cabin warmed their bodies and hearts as they occasionally touched strong movements of an unborn but lively child when Nan would alert them to this activity. Ned felt he had never known such happiness and wondered whether life could ever be so perfect in the future.

Ella found that she missed Nan intensely while the young Canes were away in Oklahoma. She had fantasies of the couple's moving to Ned's parents' to regain his roots, raise their children and never return to Flat Rock. Her fantasies turned to plans as she realized she did not want to live alone in the big Quinn house anymore. Once Ella knew what she wanted, she moved quickly to initiate first moves, offering to make a proper place of storage and safety for Tom Heath's drawings and color sketches. She offered the top floor of her farmhouse. The journals would have secure storage there, good lighting from four sides, and adequate ventilation. She decided to move chairs and tables up to the gallery for reading sessions of Tom's notes. Nan and Ned were eager to accept the space. The transfer of the art from the workshop back of the burned Heath home was done after dark in order to avoid revealing Tom's creative body of work.

Once this was accomplished, a week after Nan and Ned returned from Oklahoma, Ella decided to express her wishes that the Canes move into the farmhouse before the baby was to arrive, that Ned work with an aging Otis to run the Quinn farm, and to have her niece know the story of Ted and Lizzy's move westward. For this emotionally charged revelation the aunt decided to include Otis and Sadie in the family meeting in the large dining room with a low-burning fire appropriate for cool October evenings. On the memorable night of establishing family ties Ella presented the last will and testament of Ted Quinn along with the written wishes of Lizzy, who at the time of her writing before women's suffrage was won, was considered chattel.

Ella began.

"My parents left to me their entire estate. Otis and Sadie had been given deed to the back sixty-four acres before Bess and I were born. The will instructed me to give half of everything to my sister Bess at any such time she may be widowed or destitute, and upon my death to leave the entire estate to her, or to her children at my death if Bess should predecease me. I prefer to gift while living, and will, with formal papers, give to Nan half of all I have, including the main house and all properties. We are a family now, and with your growing family we may look forward to happiness again on our land, with the laughter of children which at my age of forty-three I shall not have myself. If you and Ned will accept my offer we all prosper by caring for each other and growing in love. Please move from that dreary place over the morgue as soon as possible! There is room for all of us here with even space in the barn for the red Cadillac!" She paused with laughter.

Nan and Ned were stunned by the offer and were unable to speak.

"There is more to tell," Ella went on.

"Only Otis, Sadie and I know of my parents' secret background in the East. My father was disowned by his father, John Quinn, because he left the priesthood. My mother was a novitiate in a convent in Savannah who, having said confessions to Father Quinn, knew, as did Ted, that they belonged together. The two left the East, just married, with a grand inheritance from Grandmother Quinn, Mary Kelley Quinn. The more complete story may be told slowly as we spend evenings between reading Tom's wonderful journals and going over Ted and Lizzy's story."

Lucky for the Canes, Ella was forced to pause for lemonade because the couple felt somewhat dazed by all the images of the past suddenly presented to them.

The aunt continued, 'I only learned of these truths at my parents' deaths when Sadie gave me the key to my father's chest and told me all she knew. Inside the private box I found father's chasuble, stole, collars, holy water vial, and a bible. Mother's headdress from the convent was also inside, with beautiful rosaries and crosses. Bess never knew but now I feel it proper that Nan know her history. She, or her children, may someday find Boston, Baltimore, or Savannah relatives. I plan to ask my father's two sisters who attempted to find him years ago to come here when your baby is born. I informed them of my parents' deaths but did not want to see them at that time. They, Kathleen and Bridget, are spinsters, who although heirs to plenty, used their intelligence to buy into the famous early Baltimore ice cream and cone business. They would be in their sixties now because father was seventy-six and mother sixty-eight when they went off the bridge on that dark night.

"And now I am drained by revealing so much, and perhaps rushed, but so much is happening so fast with an approaching new life. You two will please me by your answer's coming promptly ... if you are able to accept my proposals."

There was silence in the dining room where Sadie and Otis had been asked to pull their chairs up to the table. They sat, but not all the way up to the table.

Nan and Ned looked at each other. Immediately it was clear that living quarters, farm land, family ties, were all grand prizes. Ned smiled at Nan who hugged Sadie and Otis, and for the first time hugged Ella, placing a kiss on her forehead saying, "Yes, yes, dear Aunt. My child shall have folks! A year ago I cried out that I had no folks!"

Ella gave the second story of the house to the Canes, moving herself downstairs into quarters which had been used by her parents in their later years. Ralph Hahn did not lose Ned altogether as a much-needed assistant in preparing the dead for funerals and burials but farm work on Ralph's land would now require more help from his son-in-law. With so few possessions, Nan and Ned made the change of address quickly. Sadie, along with Ned's input in the kitchen, served up great meals, followed by readings on the third floor. Tom's notes and thoughts always stimulated discussions and varied interpretations:

"I dream of someday using color, the most capricious of visual elements, as the first import in my efforts. Presently my drawings and color sketches, initially and finally, read as form and I fear color energy will fly off the surface, leaving me helpless … perhaps flying off into spiritual planes. Rembrandt gave us results which artists work towards; results in which paint strokes determine form … paint, free of enslavement to filling in pre-established drawings. Who among us is so in tune with a personalized technique we call manner or style, a fingerprint like no other? Only geniuses? To interpret, transform, not just record, is a lifetime task toward uniqueness, which, when great, cannot be parodied. To even attempt this is to be possessed by a crazed arrogance! It is a stretch to a totally new image. I have only begun."

The notes read that night would have to be discussed another evening. Nan began to weep as she realized her father had not just begun but had ended his studio work. In this life he was lost to her forever. She wanted to believe beyond that. Throughout the night she was revisited by a grief like that which had wrapped around her the night of the fire.

Upon standing to go downstairs they saw a paper fall out of the journal. Ella stopped to pick it up and, handing it to Nan, glanced at the single paper with large writing. Her face expressed shock to match her words.

"How could you go into my drawer, Nan? This is one of my grandmother's recipes. I can't believe you have done this!!"

"Oh, no, no! That is a recipe Ned's mother gave me because it is from the kitchen of Martha Davis Seltzer, the mother of Catherine Seltzer Brown. Charlotte Cane's mother was Catherine. Mother Cane, as I call her, married David Cane and told me of their history. You are mistaken."

"What trick has God played on you or the devil rather, with evil deeds? Bess never knew that Lizzy's maiden name was Seltzer, she was the daughter of Harry Seltzer and Martha Davis Seltzer ... dear God, the sisters lived all these years only a state away. When families split ... Lizzy left Savannah and Catherine must have ended up in Oklahoma in marriage. It's just not right!!! You children have the same great grandmother ... yes, this is the exact same recipe and signed 'From the kitchen of Martha Davis, Seltzer, 1820 Savannah, Georgia.' We are somehow caught up in a web of confusion of events only possible in a wide country with folks leaving families instead of remaining in their homeland."

Ned jumped to his feet. "Well, whatever fate has dealt us, we are happy and strangely enough we have just tied family knots which came on us as surprises! There is nothing evil about our circumstances ... my mother will come to see us here and you will have gained a cousin who will love you. I am not saddened by any of this but I will see that Nan gets to bed now. Perhaps she'll recover from the evening's blows."

Nan did not recover easily but rather sat straight up in bed several times during that night, mumbling.

"Ned, I have not grieved the loss of my mother ... just my father and Katie ... my beautiful mother ... whose death was the end of my beginning. Now my child is beginning in my body ... if I died with this baby now it is the only possible human chance to die with another as one body ... we all die alone, physically. May I live to celebrate my baby's beginning ... and be forgiven by my mother for failing to truly mourn her dying. She is the one I cannot really believe is gone from me."

Descending the stairs in heavy moods and with bent

heads next morning, the Canes's spirits were changed quickly when, upon entering the kitchen, Ella greeted them.

"Come, children, and eat this great corn bread from our ancestor from Georgia. Sadie and I have already made it and it is ready to cut!"

Sadie had the big round heavy cast-iron griddle required by the recipe. She had the white lard, the white unsweetened corn meal, milk, tiny chopped onions, and finely ground pepper and salt. She knew the so-called hoe-cake must be cooked on a hot flame to darken both sides of the turned large "pie," just short of burning it, and cut into pie slices. If desired, the slice could be cut again through the flat side and stuffed with sausage or bacon. Martha had suggested … best served with grits, or to sop up redeye ham gravy. Sadie always had grits. This bread would be served throughout their lives and the lives of their children. Ella was now excited about meeting Charlotte Brown Cane and sharing the corn bread. If longevity comes from flexibility this family had recovered overnight for long lives.

After breakfast on the day of their first cutting of the cornbread together, a car drove up to the big house. Felix jumped up onto the veranda and called out to Ned who came quickly with Nan, having recognized his voice. The boy had gained weight and seemed taller, with even brighter blue eyes than they remembered. His former long golden locks had been cut to short waves, making him look older, while agility of his movements, along with a broad smile, told a story of some recovery.

Two graying figures stepped out of the new Model T Ford, introducing themselves as Felix's grandparents from Mississippi, along with a family physician who felt confident he could treat Felix's epilepsy.

"I couldn't leave Kansas without saying goodbye to the only ones who befriended me when I was so lonely in the asylum. Nan, after you quit the job Ned continued to be so kind to me. When he left too, I didn't know what would become of me ... but my grandparents came for me. They're taking me home with them."

After a warm afternoon of expressing feelings and renewing friendships, Felix drove away, loved and filled with hope. Nan could never forget the chase among the hemlocks.

Otis had his plans for using the land he had been given. With Ella's help he had put in place plans for billboards to be leased on his property along the old Trail, a rapidly growing traffic artery. The trail divided one hundred of the Quinn acres and sixty four acres which had been deeded to the Bankses. Roadside food stands for travelers had started up in Texas by 1920. Otis knew he and Sadie could run a drive-up and takeout food stand on the trail, as aging was bringing a loss of endurance for farm work. Food stands along with the billboards would prove to be a money maker. Later, Ned would lease Nan's land on the other side, along The Old Trail, to advertisers for billboards.

On the day of the presidential election, in November 1920, Ella and Nan, leaving in a new Model T Ford, were flagged down by Ned, working with Otis in a field near the drive from the main house.

"Where are you two going in the new buggy?" Ned asked.

"Well since the passing of the Amendment in August gave women the right to vote we're off for Ella to cast her first vote at the special room set up next to the Sheriff's office," Nan almost shouted with joy.

Ned teasingly replied, "Good girls!! But I believe Ella bought the new car to impress the Baltimore aunts when they come at Christmas."

"Of course not," Ella protested. "It was time to get the old Maxwell out of the barn. Besides, those women are coming to see a new baby … not a new car. You had better hope the baby is a boy because if it's a girl we will have four generations of females who could henpeck you."

"That will never happen! My mama handled a house with six men and I picked up her strength for holding my own. What's more, Nan, your mother may have said that inbreeding produces either imbeciles or geniuses, but I'm betting on a brood of brilliance for America!" Then, before turning to look back over his shoulder. Ned leaned into the car window, surprising Nan with lines from Tennyson,

Behold, we know not anything;
    I can but trust that good shall fall
    At last--far off--at last, to all,
And every winter change to spring